SNOW SHOES

Eileen Casey

SNOW SHOES

ARLEN
HOUSE

Snow Shoes

is published in 2012 by
ARLEN HOUSE
42 Grange Abbey Road
Baldoyle
Dublin 13
Ireland
Phone: +353 86 8207617
Email: arlenhouse@gmail.com
arlenhouse.blogspot.com

ISBN 978–1–85132–042–4, paperback
978–1–85132–052–3, hardback

International distribution by
SYRACUSE UNIVERSITY PRESS
621 Skytop Road, Suite 110
Syracuse, New York
USA 13244–5290
Phone: 315–443–5534/Fax: 315–443–5545
Email: supress@syr.edu
www.syracuseuniversitypress.syr.edu

Typesetting by Arlen House

Front cover artwork 'Diviner' and back cover artwork
'Out of the Blue' are by Emma Barone

CONTENTS

Acknowledgements are due the editors of *Verbal Arts Magazine* ('Dr Quirkey's Good Time Emporium'), *The Moth* ('Put Your Shoes On, Susie, We're Going Out Tonight'), New Irish Writing, *The Sunday Tribune* ('Ants' and 'Macaw'), *The Maria Edgeworth Winners' Anthology* 2005 ('That Woman') where versions of these stories first appeared. 'For Soon-Ae-Kang' was published in the *2002 Winners' Anthology*, Listowel Writers Week. 'Fuchsia' was published in *Alms on the Highway*, The Oscar Wilde Centre, Trinity College, Dublin, 2011.

For providing a creative space in which to flourish, respect is owed the 2010/2012 faculty and visiting writers on the M.Phil in Creative Writing, Oscar Wilde Centre, Trinity College, Dublin.

For her absolute commitment to the discipline of writing and for her generosity of spirit, thanks are due to Deirdre Madden.

Affection and gratitude to visual artist and dear friend Emma Barone.

Sincere gratitude to Alan Hayes for continuing to encourage and support new voices. Also, the Tyrone Guthrie Centre, Newbliss, Co. Monaghan and the Heinrich Böll Cottage Committee, Achill Island, where some of the work in *Snow Shoes* was completed.

Thanks to the Arts Council for the granting of an Individual Artist's Bursary in 2010/2011.

For my treasures; Aoife, Callum and Saoirse

SNOW SHOES

Snow Shoes

Eyes, that's what Rob needed. Lots of extra pairs. All shapes and colours. Ears too. A clone or two would be even better. He could be home at the same time as being in work. Slackening his shoulder blades, stretching taut muscles in his neck. A crash on the couch, even half an hour ... so little sleep the night before, and nothing to do with sex. A definite no-no, at least until the teething season's over. He wishes. Tracy looking pale and gaunt didn't help him on his way to work. Or the car. The engine making that awful whine when he turned the ignition. More stress, more bills.

Henry's voice from the 'control room', a cubby hole behind the vegetable aisle, crackles through Rob's earphones. 'This is Captain Kirk calling Security. Mother Ship to base. Klingon Thompson's heading your way, over'. Holding his arms rigid at his sides, Rob stares straight ahead, his face impassive. He's not fooled for a minute by Henry's Klingon warning or his all lads together cosy routine. Henry's on his fat arse for most of the day while Rob's on his feet. Taking up position at the front entrance is his least favourite duty. A gust of cold air blows on his face every time the automatic door opens but being a Monday, and with the bad weather, shoppers have thinned since the Christmas rush. Late January snow on the pavement outside is partly frozen but slushy too.

When Lee-Ann Thompson comes into view, wire basket across her arm and dressed in her 'drab ordinary housewife' clothes, he doesn't show the slightest hint of recognition. 'Blowing my cover', was how she'd described the smile and friendly nod he'd given her, barely a week in the job. It's a lot stricter here than his last stint for sure, the hours in the warehouse passing without seeing a living soul. And bored out of his tree but at least he could play his own kind of music then and not have to listen to a constant stream of schmaltzy crap played for pensioners and housewives. Sedation music. So no-one gets too excited buying the cornflakes. Lee-Ann gives him a coy glance and moves on, her rubber soles soundless on the tiled floor. She might be his own age, early thirties. It's hard to know with women like her, all make up and no ties, arriving into work in tight skirts and high heels, changing into 'flats', doing her best to look like a 'drab ordinary housewife', going about the business of shopping for her 'average' family. Rob is sure she'd include Tracy in those categories, just because she's housebound with a baby.

Despite himself, his eyes are drawn to where Lee-Ann strolls among the rails of sweaters and colour coded jackets. Handbags and shoes are stacked on shelves near the accessories and she sometimes fingers a scarf all casual like or spreads it across her shoulders, posing in front of one of the full length mirrors, as if seriously considering buying it. 'I wouldn't wear the tat they sell here if my life depended on it', Rob's often heard her say to Audrey, the red-head from the off-licence.

Every time he looks up at the huge clock face over the Customer Services desk, the hands barely seem to have stirred. When he moves away from the entrance doors and begins his tour of duty there's no sign of Lee-Ann. He guesses she might be deep in coded conversation, pretending to buy wine or a bottle of sherry. The check-out ladies nod to him from their perch behind the tills. Sometimes, women on the check-outs take turns to work on the shop-floor when they aren't busy and he sometimes helps them sort through the returns from the changing rooms or the jumbles of clothes knocked from the rails.

'Hey Rob, give us a hand', Big Myra calls to him as he passes by Ladies' Fashions. 'Sure, I've got all the time in the world', he says, picking up a blouse and a clothes hanger from Myra's trolley.

'Some of the customers are pigs, eh', she says, sorting the clothes by size. Myra moves her large arms as if in slow motion, an expert in stretching out a fifteen minute job to fill the guts of an hour. A study in time and no motion.

'Where's Mandy today, there's no sign of her?' Rob asks, draping the newly hung blouse over the handles of the trolley.

'Did you not hear? Her house got done yesterday in broad daylight. She'd only nipped to the shops and they were in and out by the time she came back. She's in shock. All their wedding presents robbed. And the money that was put by for the credit union. There'll be no Tenerife now'. Myra purses her mouth until it's a crumpled, thin line. 'You'd wonder why we bother working when there's nothing but thugs around every corner, waiting to pounce the minute our back's turned'. Rob nods but says nothing. Myra's worked in the store so long he thinks she must be institutionalised and no amount of robberies would shift her. She picks up the clothes he's already re-hung and checks that the buttons are closed and the shoulders are straight.

Mid-morning comes at last. Rob removes his ear phones and heads into the tea-room for his break. The room is standard Formica and chrome, with scuffed lino and a window that faces out into a yard full of empty wooden pallets at the back of the store. There are still wisps of tinsel straggling from some of the notices, looking sad and tired. 'Captain Henry Kirk', sleeves rolled up and heavily perspiring despite the cold in the room, calls a 'Hi Rob, catch any Romulans yet?' Rob shakes his head, playing along though he hasn't a clue what time-warp Henry's trapped in. 'What do you make of this?' Henry asks, pointing to the newspaper spread out before him on the table. Take a look; it's the best I've seen in a long while'.

'What is it? Rob asks, pretending interest. He thinks better of plugging in the kettle until Henry finishes reading out the item. Henry reaches for his glasses and wipes the paper free of digestive biscuit crumbs. 'According to this, some poor bastard's been found up a mountain someplace out foreign, frozen to death and face down in the snow'.

'Nothing strange there, is there?' Rob replies, 'People are discovered on mountains all the time, killing themselves for the glory of reaching the top'. Rob gives the kettle a shake, checking for water before he switches it on.

'No Rob my lad, you don't understand', Henry says. 'He was found in a fancy designer suit and wearing new shoes, not a mark on them, nothing. Here, read it yourself if you don't believe me. Frozen solid when they found him, can you believe it?'

Rob takes the paper from Henry's outstretched hand and tucks it under his arm as the kettle begins to boil, piercing the air with its shrill whistle. He warms his mug and then pops in a teabag, leaving it to brew before finally taking a seat and shaking out the tabloid. There's a picture of an ice-capped peak in Mallnitz, Austria, and a large headline 'Dressed to Chill' about a designer body being found, some copy writer's idea of a joke.

'Yeah, looks like it's true alright', Rob says, reading quickly through the couple of paragraphs under the photograph of the peak in Mallnitz. 'Wonder how he got there? Probably flung from a plane like it says there somewhere. Drug barons most like. Sure what's new?' He closes the page and folds the paper neatly, adding as an afterthought, 'Maybe he's a fallen angel or come from another planet, like Newton. Henry looks at him with a blank expression, 'Who the fuck's Newton?'

'Forget it, it doesn't matter', Rob says. Jesus, what planet did Henry come from? Everyone knew who Newton was didn't they?

'Who the fuck's Newton?' Henry asks again. 'Is he of Newton and Ridley by any chance?' He looks rattled so Rob says, 'It's never too early to talk beer but if you're not a Bowie fan, no sweat. It's just some stupid film that's all, *The Man who Fell to Earth*. About an alien coming to earth who never makes it home again'.

'Why's that, is he killed by the Mafia or what?' Henry says, slabbing together two digestives and dunking them into his tea.

'No, he takes a mistress, becomes a drunk and soon forgets about his wife and child left behind on a dying planet', Rob explains. He doesn't think Henry would be interested in the finer points.

'Nothing new there either', Henry says with a shrug. 'There's plenty would play away if they got the chance. Maybe that's what happened to Newton here. Anyway, time for the Captain to step down from the bridge. I'm going for a cigarette'. He scrapes back his chair, leaving his cup on the table amid the coffee rings and crumbs. 'The cleaners get well over the odds to do it', he often says. As usual, Henry's left the milk carton lid off, and as usual, when Rob pours milk into his own mug, he tightens it back on again. It's the one thing that drives Tracy crazy so he's well trained on that score. Rob sips at his tea and thinks about his day off on Wednesday, a psychological break which makes the week seem shorter. At least that's what he's telling himself. If it's not too cold maybe they could go somewhere but deep down he knows that's not going to happen. Most of the day will be spent catching up on sleep. He spreads out the newspaper on the table, his eyes again drawn to the caption about the grisly find. He wonders how long the man was lying there, his face buried in hard packed snow, his skin hardening by the hour. All that silence in a frozen world. And so random. Anything could happen and when least expected.

As he stirs two spoons of sugar into his tea he remembers his conversation with Myra. It's the broad daylight feature of the robbery that's beginning to knaw at him. He takes a larger gulp of the liquid than intended, the extra volume scalding the inside of his mouth. Even the sting of the burn can't rid him of the image of a burglar breaking into his house. Tracy might be out at the shops but he doesn't think so, the weather is cold and the paths are slippery. She'll more than likely be at home innocently washing a pile of laundry or brushing the sweeper over the brown carpet in the living room, Monday being the day for hovering and washing. Maybe the break-in's happening at this very moment while he's here drinking tea and eating a stale digestive. Owen, sleeping through it all, or worse, woken up and crying while his father's in a stupid department store miles away in the city centre. A step up from his last Security job but hardly World Enterprises.

'You look as if you've seen a ghost', Lee-Ann says, coming into the room. He shrugs his shoulders and shakes his head. 'Just needed a brew, that's all'. Again, he sips at the tea; it's cooler now and when he places the mug back on the table he wraps his hands around it.

'Hang-over eh?' Lee-Ann says. He doesn't reply. It's been a while since he's had a session but he's not going to tell her that. You'll never guess the latest scam', Lee-Ann continues, sliding her tall, skinny frame into the nearest chair. He's never seen her take tea or coffee or any kind of food, at least not on his breaks anyway. Although she's super slim, he has also noticed her super size breasts pushing against her jumper. He inclines his head in her direction, careful to keep his eyes on her face at all times.

'I just caught a very respectably dressed, middle-aged geezer with a very swanky accent switching that expensive toothpaste, you know the one for sensitive gums? Well, he swapped it into a cheaper packet. I wouldn't have noticed him doing it only I decided to take a look down the toiletries aisle and there he was, his head darting around, real guilty like'.

'Maybe he wasn't himself, people do strange things under pressure', Rob says.

'No fear he put the cheap one into the expensive packet then, now that's what I'd call distracted'. Lee-Ann rubs the backs of her long legs and flexes her shoulders. 'Christ, that basket can weigh heavy after a while. I'll be taking the trolley express for the afternoon; it's great for leaning on'. She takes out a shiny compact from her jacket pocket, clicks open the clasp and stares at her face, fluffing up her hair with her free hand, checking that her lipstick's still on. Her lips are full, her teeth white and even. Lee-Ann catches him staring at her mouth and slips her tongue between her teeth, then peers into the mirror again, searching her eyes for smudged mascara or a stray eyelash. Finally, she snaps the compact shut. She returns his stare and he quickly looks down, examining his fingernails.

'It's pretty genius though isn't it?' Rob says at last, 'Who'd think of it? What'll happen to him now? Did he get off with a warning?'

'Did he hell!' Lee-Ann shoots back, her eyes widening with outrage. 'I pretended to be a packer at the check-out and accidentally let the toothpaste fall out of the packet. The look on his face did the rest of the work. I never saw anyone as scared in all my life. Blabbing like a baby at his age'. Lee-Ann makes a grimace of disgust. Rob wants to say that she could have let him off with a warning, that times were tough if a man couldn't afford toothpaste for sensitive gums. But that was Lee-Ann, cold as ice.

'Better get back', he says, rising from the table, taking his mug to the sink, washing, rinsing, drying and then putting it back in its place in the cabinet.

'Who's a good boy then?' Lee-Ann laughs a teasing laugh that follows him all the way out of the room.

'Kirk here', Henry's voice crackles as Rob begins yet another tour of the store. He's eaten his sandwiches, corn beef and brown sauce, a one time favourite he's now tiring of. The sandwiches might satisfy his hunger but his taste buds could do with a holiday.

'He can't have been dumped from a plane', Henry is saying, his tone smug.

'Who?' Rob says into his mouthpiece. He's getting fed up with Henry's Captain Kirk routine making out they're best mates when the truth was, one false move and Rob would be out the door. Okay for Henry, in his cushy job, nothing to do but watch monitors and make up rosters. His family probably all grown up too so he could afford to be on the couch half the night watching re-runs on channels Rob's never even heard of.

'That Newton gentleman in the designer suit and fancy shoes, that's who', Henry says.

'Okay, so why couldn't he have been dumped from a plane', Rob replies, annoyed by Henry's familiarity with a character from a film he's never heard of until a few hours ago. 'Because his hat was still on, that's why... over and out'. Henry's self satisfied exit is a further irritant for Rob. The detail of the hat meant squat. So what? The guy could easily have replaced it when he landed in the snow, proving he probably wasn't even dead when he was dumped.

When Rob passes the furniture section, he sees a couple he guesses to be in their late teens bounce onto the wide bed that boasts an orthopaedic mattress. The girl wears bright coloured socks that go all the way to her knees and he can see a white stripe of thigh as she turns into the boy for a quick kiss. Rob knows he'll have to warn them off the bed if they go too far but thankfully the girl spots him and they bounce off again, laughing at each other, scrambling for their shoes.

He walks through the freezer part of the supermarket section adjacent to clothes and furniture. It's part of his daily routine to check that the fridges are working or there's nothing spilled on the floor that might bring a compensation claim. Cleaners give the store the once over early in the morning but the things people did, just for pushing out the boundaries, seeing how far they could go. Twisting the caps off soft drinks for one thing, taking quick swigs and putting the bottles back again, leaving the caps loose. Eating stock without paying for it is fairly common. The night packers regularly find half eaten bars of chocolate and packets of biscuits at the backs of the shelves. Those culprits could hardly be accused of shop lifting. He wonders why Lee-Ann hasn't thought of using a stomach pump to prove in-store eating.

'Be a presence, let people know they can't get one over on you', Henry told him on his first day, three months ago. So far so good, nothing major has happened on his shifts. He knows the local winos now and all he has to do is refuse them entry and make sure they didn't loiter around the entrance. There are gangs of professional lifters too. Brazen as anything and hard-faced with it. Sometimes they slip the net but he's nabbed a couple of convictions so earns his keep. He's still not sorry to have been off work the week before when Lee-Ann caught a young woman with nappies under the apron of her pram, bragging about it to Audrey in the tea-room. Walking past the freezers loaded with frozen foods, he's glad of his heavy jumper. At least he doesn't have to re-stock this section every Friday and can't imagine how the packers manage to keep moving, for all their thermal jackets. That man found up the mountain must have been dumped from a plane for sure though and definitely alive. He couldn't have stood a chance in the cold, especially only wearing a designer suit. The thought of the freezing temperatures shutting down all his senses sends a chill. He'd heard hearing's the last to go. And so weird about his shoes, not a mark on them. One cool dude alright, even if a dead one. Whatever he'd done must have pissed someone off.

Shoes. He's noticed that a lot of the customers are wearing snow grips on their shoes when they come into the store, removing them at the entrance. Held over the toes and heels, they look just like rubber bands with a spiky grip on them to avoid slipping. Some bright spark came up with the idea, probably making a fortune now in all the bad weather. Rob wishes he'd thought of it, all those hours on night shifts with nothing to do. Such a simple idea too. Why couldn't he have thought of it? Maybe he should get a pair for Tracy? The ice wouldn't be such a problem then. At least there'd be a good chance she'd be out of the house if a burglar does decide to come calling. But he doesn't know where to buy them and he hasn't seen them anywhere on display in the store.

He takes up position once more at the entrance doors. A rush of school uniforms barge through, the after school pile-up of 'acne and testosterone', Lee-Ann calls it. Girls pretending to choose a deodorant, spraying it all over the aisle; boys heading towards the cold drinks and crisps on their way towards the rear exit which leads them into the main shopping mall. They're a blur of faces. But to them he's invisible, they're not one bit intimidated by him. He probably looks like a joke to them, all togged out in heavy Security gear and earphones. Some are holding hands, the beginning of first love. His mind drifts to his heavily mortgaged three bedroom-semi miles from the city. If only they'd rented first, they could walk away now. Without even a scuff mark.

'Mother ship to base, mother ship to base, do you read me ... over'. Henry's voice startles him. Rob would give anything to tell him where to go with his mother ship to base shite. But he clears his throat and says, 'Yeah, I read you, over'.

'Those school kids, keep an eye on them, they're swarming around the CD's. A pile of them went missing last week'.

'But they're all tagged', Rob argues. Nevertheless, he moves forward towards the music aisle. Sure enough, he sees a batch of school uniforms so he decides to humour Henry and stand at the top of the aisle. Some of the girls give him the two fingers and walk off. Rob wonders where 'Klingon' Thompson is. Part of him wants the kids to stuff their pockets and get one over on her but chance would be a fine thing. Soon, they grow bored and move away, onto greener pastures in the arcade nearby.

Rob heads once again to the entrance. He's on the home stretch, the last hour. His gaze travels to the wire mat just inside the plate glass frontage of the automatic doors. Saturated since the weekend, it reminds him of an overflowing bathtub, oozing liquid each time a shopper squelches onto it. Tracy sometimes takes a bath in the middle of the afternoon, the water hot as she can bear it, gushing in, swirling like leaves around the scented soap petals or salts she sprinkles in. He thinks of the hot scented water, only it's not Tracy's face he's seeing but Lee-Ann's and it's definitely not Tracy's body that emerges in the steamy waters. He shakes the image away and leans against the wall. He can barely make out Henry's 'Mother ship to base, Klingon Thompson's got a suspect, Mother ship to base, over …'

Across a stretch of cream and brown tiles he sees Lee-Ann heading in his direction. Her eyes are trained on the back of a young woman wheeling a buggy. He recognises her from earlier on in the afternoon when he retrieved the soother her toddler flung from his buggy in a fit of pre-sleep crankiness. But he knows the drill. Lee-Ann gives him the nod and moves back into the store. It's down to Rob now to follow the suspect outside and apprehend her, take her to Henry's office where the guards will be called before a full search and interrogation. The young woman steps outside, Rob tips her on the elbow. She turns around and he sees the dark circles under her eyes.

'I've reason to believe you have goods not paid for', he says, pointing to the shopping tray under the buggy.

'But I've not bought anything', she explains. 'These are mine, I'll show you'. Red-faced, she bends down and fumbles with the knot on a plastic bag. Rob sees the jar of nappy cream and the bottle of baby oil wedged underneath. She removes a pair of snow shoes from the bag and hands them to him. His ear phones begin to crackle but so faint the sound could be coming from a long way off. He weighs up his options. He could ask the young woman to come back into the store with him, get a pat on the back from Henry and a sly smile from Lee-Ann … Or say he must be mistaken? He looks up at the blank screen of the sky, turning over the plastic, pressing steel grips into the soft flesh of his palm.

The Genuine Article

The queue seems longer than usual for a Friday mid-afternoon. Anna is in two minds but the need to collect her pension nudges her over the threshold. The interior of the post office is cool at least, with its tiled floor, high ceiling. Sunlight, like an unwelcome visitor seldom gets past the four thick stone steps at the front door.

Scarcely has Anna taken her place at the end of the line when Molly Dunne comes in behind her.

'Terrible about that poor man, isn't it? Who'd credit it?' Molly says without any ceremony. Anna half turns and nods to the woman she's known for over thirty years and still cannot bear the sight of.

'Yes, it's frightening. He wasn't that old really', Anna says.

'You never know the minute or the hour you'll be planted', Molly continues, raising her voice, wanting to include anyone within earshot. 'And on such a hot day!' she adds with relish. 'Even the milk's turning'. Molly clicks her tongue against the roof of her mouth like a clucking hen and folds her arms across her wide girth. 'Have you been up to Finn's yet?' Molly asks after a slight pause. Myself and Eddy went yesterday. Talk about a crowd! Hardly room to stir. I suppose he knew a lot of people from going around in that old van'.

Anna shakes her head. No, she hasn't been to the undertakers. Her stomach churns, half in guilt, half in sorrow for the man who'd lived two doors down from her.

'I'm surprised to hear that, thought you'd be one of the first there … you living so close to him and all', she hastily explains, giving Anna a sly look. 'You'll have to hurry', she continues, her tone slightly more sombre, 'They'll be screwing down the lid in a few hours. That's the last light that poor man will ever see'. Molly sets her face in an expression of mock sympathy.

Anna turns her back as the queue inches forward. Anger stirs in the pit of her stomach. A hypocrite, that's what Molly is for sure. As far as Anna's aware, there's been little or no recent exchange except a nod of the head between Molly and Raymond, the dead man. Not since the transactions at Molly's front door, years ago now, when he'd collect the weekly instalments for whatever item had been bought from the back of his blue Bedford van.

'The Jew man', Molly christened him. 'Writing everything down in his little red notebooks'. Anna knew that others called him that also, but they were still glad to be able to buy goods from him they didn't have to pay off in a lump sum. House-hold goods, pots and pans, towels and bedclothes. Anna wonders if Molly is one of those who still owe him money, suddenly glad she herself had paid up for accounts promptly and had everything squared before he finally called it a day on his haberdashery travelling shop. The arrival of the shopping centres in the nearest big towns and the opening of Fayle's hardware out near the roundabout put money in the pockets of those who, before that, couldn't get work and also meant prices Raymond couldn't compete with.

Nearing the counter at last Anna once more turns back to face Molly.

'I'm not sure if I'll go to Finn's or not, maybe it's best to remember him as he was', she says. Deep down however, she knows she will go.

'He looks terrible, not a jot of colour, his whole face drained', Molly says, again raising her voice to include anyone that cares to join in or that might know the man she is talking about. 'And neither chick nor child to mourn him'. Then, unable to resist, she adds, 'As far as we can tell. Who knows who'll come crawling out of the woodwork now he's snuffed it? He must have covered half the country in that blue van and that house is surely his, lock, stock and barrel. What will become of it now?'

She looks Anna full in the eye but Anna returns the stare and does not flinch. No-one else responds. A bored looking teenager blows out a chewing gum bubble that nearly covers her face and then snaps it back into her mouth again with practiced ease. The queue moves along quickly enough and before long, to her immense relief, Anna winds up her business at the counter and is out on the street again.

She could head in either of two directions but she walks towards Finn's which is tucked away on a side street that connects through a laneway with the middle of the town. The shops are at the height of their busiest period, the last couple of hours before the awnings are rolled up and the shutters pulled down. Shoppers weave along the pavements, a mix of townspeople and farmers with their wives in search of hardware items, feed for stock and provisions for the week. A young man and woman lounge outside the video shop waiting for it to open. Smoke billows an acrid smell from their cigarettes. They barely break apart to let her pass; laughter follows her down the street.

Anna finds it hard not to envy the young women their skimpy tops and short skirts. Some of them are pushing toddlers and babies in buggies or prams. They wear strong shades of lipstick and their stiletto heels clack along the pavement making slim legs look even longer than they are. Friday is dole day so there's extra money for spending. Country and Western music drifts out the open doorway of a public house. The tang of fish and chips wafting from the town's one and only fast food outlet near Power's Bookie's reminds her she still needs to shop for dinner. Sunlight jumps off the rows of cars parked all along both sides of the street and shimmers on the cider flagons gripped by the small band sprawled across the base of the large stone war memorial. She recognises one or two of the drinkers. Some of them, to her knowledge, never once left the town.

Although dressed as lightly as she can for her years, Anna still feels cloistered up in her long cream coloured dress. She loosens the top buttons of her dress but baulks at taking off her cardigan. Her dress has short sleeves and her arms are flabby like the neck of a turkey. But it's so hot. In the window of the vegetable shop she notices how even the fruit and vegetables are all dried up, shrunken. The meat in the butcher shop window is a funny shade too. Despite the fly catchers suspended from the ceiling a number of insects crawl along the fatty surface of chops and half legs of lamb that are mottling into the brownish speckled colour of tainted meat.

She crosses the street to walk through the lane that will take her to Finn's, pausing for a moment to look into what used to be Coyne's Drapery shop window. Of course, it's called a boutique now, the youngest of the Coyne's coming back from America and modernising it to move forward with the times. Mannequins wearing tiny bikinis and large brimmed sunhats stand beside striped deckchairs and rolled out towels. Anna smiles despite herself. There'd be more than a few turning in their graves.

Her footsteps are a little lighter as she makes her way up the lane, arriving at Finn's just as someone she doesn't recognise is leaving. Molly was probably right concerning the amount of people Raymond must have known all those years of being on the road. When she pushes open the door of the funeral parlour she could be on a different planet. Air conditioning rushes out to cool her. Liturgical chant filters around her.

The reception area is also an office but it's fitted out like a study so the business end of the whole undertaking transactions are low-key. There's a smell of leather and the carpet pile is deep enough to cushion the heaviest step. A blonde haired secretary in a smart blouse and light jacket sits behind a mahogany desk, as big as a dining table, full of Mass card paraphernalia and the inevitable forms. Anna thinks she's one of the Middleton girls, the youngest. She has the bony look of her mother Rita, but she can't be sure it's her and she won't ask.

The secretary looks up, her mouth widening just enough that the smile is welcoming but also striking the right note of sympathy. Anna nods back and asks where she might pay her respects to the deceased.

'The remains are two doors down the corridor on the left hand side, Madam', the secretary replies just as the phone detonates the austere atmosphere and is picked up on the second ring. As she walks away Anna can hear the low hum of the conversation but doesn't quite catch what's being said. The secretary has been very polite, in an old fashioned way, calling Anna 'Madam'. In deference to her age perhaps, considering her to be a potential customer. After all, the corpse laid out down the corridor is younger than Anna and as Molly says, 'No-one knows the minute or the hour'. Joe was waked at home, his last wishes. But she'd kept the house private, just herself and the immediate family, Joe's sister Sadie and her own brother James. Even Molly Dunne hadn't dared try to get past Sadie who was well known for her acid tongue and withering glance.

Inside the viewing room, the walls are plain and painted a muted shade of green. Only the sound of a faint whirring from an overhead fan disturbs the silence. Anna supposes that in this line of business there'd have to be air conditioning, especially during high summer. Thanks to the whirling fan, she's beginning to feel less bloated. Excessive heat always does that to her. Swells her like a balloon, makes her conscious of her thighs rubbing together, the perspiration trickling down her legs like melting ice-cream. As a young woman so many years ago now it seems like it never happened, Anna was so slim she could have fitted through the eye of a needle, as the saying went. Except for her one pregnancy of course. She was lucky nowadays to fit through the door of her council house or the supermarket or the bingo hall where she spent most Thursday afternoons with her best friends from the street, Doreen and Susan. But for now it feels like she's in the middle of a forest enclosed in this cocoon of air conditioning. Were it not of course for Raymond, a corpse of just two days.

Anna draws nearer to the open casket, a lump rising in her belly. What is it? Not fear surely. Hasn't she known him well enough? Spoken to him often, been in his car, taken lifts from the shops to the street where they both lived. Rolled the r of his name around her mouth when he'd first introduced himself all those years ago.

'Raymond', he'd said, 'Chandler', she'd joked back to him, delighted when he was able to pick up on it. 'Love those books', he'd said immediately. A young man he was then, with about a decade between them Anna reckoned that first morning when he'd knocked on her door.

A Monday it was, laundry day. She'd just plugged in the iron and had the bowl of water at the ready to sprinkle over Joe's shirts, so the iron would ease over the creases more easily. Joe was so fussy about his shirts and she supposed she couldn't fault him for that. He had to look the part as manager of the men's department in Coyne's drapery store. She'd been in her shabbiest skirt and blouse when the doorbell rang, her hair all over the place. Yet Raymond smiled as if the sight of her had turned on a light. It had been a long time since anyone looked at her like that. She recognised him as the man who'd moved into the street two doors down, single as far as she could see, with a blue van parked outside. The van was gone most of the time except for the week or so before when she'd seen it at the kerb.

'Can I interest you in an oriental rug', he said, opening a folder with pictures of beautiful, colourful, exotic looking rugs.

'I don't think so', she replied, pointing to the roof above her. 'The guttering is in bad need of repair and I think anything extra will go towards that'.

'The guttering can be repaired or replaced anytime, but when will you get the chance to own an original oriental rug for such a price? And the genuine article'.

His spiel was good. As it tripped off his tongue and his hands flicked through the plastic sheeted folder, she became fascinated. A rug, no matter which one she chose, would indeed look nice in her front room. It would transform it, make it cosy. The colours were bright yet subtle and some of the patterns held the outline of a bird of paradise in the centre. The edges were fringed in silken threads of creamy silk. Why shouldn't she have something nice for a change? And she could pay for it over a whole four months. Plus she had the deposit already saved for the gutter replacement. She thought about Joe and what he might say and her enthusiasm wavered a little. Raymond saw her hesitate and took out his notebook and pen, taking down her name.

'I'll bring you samples next week and let you judge the weave for yourself', he said, giving her a wink. 'Think about it, this rug will be the making of your home and a nice heirloom for your children'.

Anna doesn't think that her son Philip will want an oriental rug if anything happens to her. The years have borne that out. Hard cash, now that would be a different proposition. He was his father's son alright. Doing well in London the last she'd heard but she didn't think he'd be coming home any time soon, considering the hurry he'd left in.

'There's nothing for me here Ma', he'd said and, deep in her heart she knew he was right.

Anna looks down into the casket finding it hard to believe that the husk of a human being she sees there has anything to do with that young man of all those years ago who came back the following week with small squares of samples as promised, and the week after that again; carried up her garden path a rolled up rug covered in protective plastic. She wonders if Molly got one too but doesn't think so. She certainly never said. With the squad of children she had, items of a more practical nature were probably more in her line.

Her own rug was still almost as good as new, faithfully taken out each summer and hung over the clotheshorse in a shady part of the garden. All the dust was gently swatted out of it with a clean brush and then a damp sponge run over it. It was lovely to see the colours brighten again. She especially liked to look at it on winter nights or when Joe was in his humours and a black cloud of silence descended over the house. At Christmas time with the fire lit and the fender shining, she'd sit in the room and admire the flames flickering over her oriental rug. The mantelpiece with the retirement clock Joe got from Coyne's was dusted down regularly. Even this morning, she'd carefully lifted it, slid her chammy over the wood and replaced it in its exact spot. Then, with even greater care she replaced the yet unopened envelope with Raymond's handwriting that had come through the door shortly before he was taken to the Hospice three towns away.

Anna blesses herself, the words of a familiar prayer springing to her lips. She hasn't been inside a church for years but like riding a bicycle it all comes back. Molly was right about the colour being drained from Raymond's face. Tall and muscular with big hands and feet, it always surprised Anna when he opened his mouth and she heard the inner city in his voice and not the broad vowels of a countryman.

'Whatever brought you to a quiet place like this?' Anna once asked him but he'd been evasive, said he preferred the quiet and that he could go around the countryside easier. I never liked the city anyway', he said. 'And where I lived the neighbours wouldn't talk to you'.

The man in the casket is not the man who said those words. He has a grotesque appearance, his face misshapen, with disfigured, distorted features. It was the invasion of the tumour that did it. Pushing out his bones, inflating his cheeks, blowfish size with the amount of drugs taken to fight it. Drugs that were no match for it in the end. She had spoken to him once or twice about it when he was in the early stages of his illness, when he was able to look death in the eye and think he could win. The bright light of his blue eyes was well and truly extinguished also, trapped forever under tight, grey coloured lids.

The memory of Raymond leaning over the gate comes to her. His shirt sleeves rolled up, showing big brawny arms, no hint of fear in his voice as he told her that he would be getting treatment but he'd be right as rain before she could say, 'Cock Robin'.

'I'll outlast that rug I sold you', he said, after she assured him that she still had it and that the years had neither worn nor frayed it. He'd smiled and the warmth reached his eyes.

'It's the genuine article', she said. He seemed pleased that it had survived the years.

'And the guttering still got repaired', he said and they'd both laughed. There'd never been any awkwardness between them.

Anna looks away from the lifeless face in the casket, willing herself to remember this man in life. How quickly his spirit has fled, as if it has slipped through the tiniest chink separating this world from the next. Anna likes to think of this passing as simply going from one space to another and shedding all care and worry in the process. All those guilty feelings and accusations, fears and reproaches, shucked off, dropping away like layers of clothing.

The funeral parlour swims back into focus. Plain walls, the same shade of green as in the reception area, with the standard crucifix nailed on. It all comes back to that in the end. Whether funeral parlour or hospital mortuary. Nothing remotely creative here, nothing to distract the eye. Two chairs are strategically placed for elderly relatives to sit and catch their mourning breaths. Or for a wife cum widow overcome with despair. Only Raymond had never married. 'Doomed to be a bachelor boy for the rest of my days', he'd often said.

A ripple from the air conditioning passes over the white frill of the satin-lined casket and it looks as if Raymond is taking in a suck of breath. Anna feels her heart rise up and lodge in her throat. For a brief moment the whole room startles into movement, even the chairs are full of shape, colours of a summer dress and bright sandals flash into her head, she gets a smell in her nostrils she can't quite identify. A floral smell, fresh, intoxicating. But it's only the air conditioning. These flashes of life disappear as quickly as they've come. She realises with a start however that outside this room, people are getting their hair done, licking lollipops, buying meat or thin shoes. People are either coming home or going out to work. Lifting telephones or mobiles and making arrangements for the evening. She herself has no plans; other than a night in front of the television or going through the paper. Where had the years flown? Only yesterday it seemed, Raymond too was at the height of his powers.

It was on the third week of the first month of paying off the instalments that Anna invited him in to see the rug laid out in its full splendour in the front room, the 'good' room, the room that had a brass fender around the fireplace and a framed print of *The Angelus* over the mantle.

'What did I say, wasn't I right?' he said, circling the rug. Be careful with sparks from the grate, you won't want to ruin it with a burn'.

'We only light the fire in here at Christmas or really special occasions', she said. She could feel her face beginning to redden. Joe preferred to sit by the range in the kitchen most nights, reading the paper or listening to the radio. Anna doesn't tell Raymond about the ructions the rug caused between her and Joe, how she begged and pleaded with him not to roll it up and bring it down to Raymond's front door, demanding back the deposit.

'What came over you woman? What about the guttering?' Joe said, over and over. 'You can nearly see the crows through the holes in it'. But she'd stuck to her guns.

Each Tuesday afternoon she looked forward to the familiar knock on the door. She wore just a trace of lipstick. Her eyes were light coloured and she was pale but she made sure her hair was washed and that her face was dusted with powder and there was a spray of perfume behind her ears and on her wrists.

'Won't be long now', he'd say as the weeks went by. 'Won't be long and then you'll be free and clear'. Anna wasn't sure if she wanted to be free and clear. Vague feelings of unease came over her at odd hours. Joe was so busy at work with the winter stock and the days were long. It didn't take much to get the house to rights.

A Tuesday soon after, Raymond came to the door as usual. It had been raining heavily on and off and she could see he was soaked through.

'Would you like to come in and warm yourself by the range, maybe take a cup of tea?' she asked, ignoring the blood flowing into her cheeks.

'That'd be great. I don't mind admitting that today hasn't been the best. I drove over sixty miles and not a sniff of a sale. Maybe I should call it and day and cut my losses'.

Anna could smell the damp on his coat and another scent that made her hands shake a little as she scoured the teapot with boiling water. 'Here, take off that wet coat and dry yourself with this', she said, handing him the towel. He removed his coat and took it from her, his large hands brushing against hers. The kitchen seemed to darken as he stood over her and she reeled a little in the small space between them.

Anna looks down at Raymond's ravaged face and remembers how he tried to keep up a brave appearance these last months and all the while his body growing its betrayal. A tumour that would spread through his organs like a plague. The way Joe had grown his own unique brand of poison; his insides eaten up with jealousy, twisting him into knots of accusation. Thank God Raymond never had any inkling of what was being said only two doors up from him.

'Molly Dunne saw that fellah's van outside our door. An hour or more he was here. I've a good mind to roll up that rag and give it back to him', he said. But her mind was made up.

'Either that rug stays or I'll go'. The extent of her anger surprised both of them.

Anna looks down at Raymond's intertwined hands. She sees how the skin is a pale grey colour. She notices too that the nails are shiny and manicured. The undertaker has been thorough. But the short hairs on his hands look stiff like a porcupine, devoid of life, of the silk threads of living. The urge to touch the skin becomes a fascination. She reaches out, making contact with the icy shock of the dead man's body. It's like touching set concrete. Nothing like the soft touch of his mouth as it rested briefly on hers. Once the initial embarrassment was over, she kissed him back. She led him into the good room and lay down for him on the rug he'd sold her and that she had almost paid for, with only three more instalments to go. The one and only regret she'd had was that it hadn't happened sooner.

The lid of the casket is propped against the wall. It looks much bigger than the actual casket itself which is a beautiful light wood colour. Not dark but golden, like honey. Etched with the cross of suffering onto the lid. As if anyone could forget for even one moment that this man is definitely gone to another outpost. Raymond's bare head is the colour of putty, a funny colour the older ones like herself will say, crossing themselves, glad it's him the grim reaper has come for and not themselves. There has been some attempt to paper over the ravages of pain with make-up but the effort hasn't been totally successful.

Anna again tries to pray, tries to re-activate old habits. Her mouth gropes along the words but she isn't able to put meaning into them. She feels a bit hypocritical really. She can't remember the last time she'd been inside a church. What was the use of her prayers now anyway?

She rises stiffly, her joints complaining. Arthritis for sure. Her mother had been crippled with it. Anna moves to the side of the casket and looks down one last time. Raymond is wearing a pearl grey suit. She's never seen it on him but then, there was so much of his world she knew nothing about. The lure of touching the hands with a rosary woven through waxen fingers proves overwhelming. Again, the contact is rock solid cold. But it's time to go. She will write her name in the Visitor's Book so that those who come after her will know that she's paid these final respects. Just an old neighbour, unsteady on her feet, fat and bloated from the heat. A woman you would pass by on the street without a second glance. She takes one last look in the casket and turns away.

DR QUIRKEY'S GOOD TIME EMPORIUM

Ann rarely leaves the shopping centre without looking at the notices pinned with white thumb tacks to the back of a long, wide glass case. Postcard or poster sized notices, all securely under lock and key. This seems to give an added importance to them plus the fact that the spaces have to be rented, not like the ones in Tescos or Dunnes that are mostly missing or found dogs or cats.

Man with Transet Van catches her eye. 'No job too big or too small'. Only the word doesn't look right. Maybe Mr Transit Van Man should be getting in touch with the notice alongside him, the one that says *Having trouble reading or spelling?* But she reckons he wouldn't need spelling to come to her house and take away all the rubbish she's gathered around herself for the last twenty five years, plus. A nice man he'll be, with a clean shirt and fingernails. He'll be wearing white gloves and a white suit when he calls to clear the decks, a bit like visiting a crime scene. 'I've come to clear your mess missus', he'll say, his eyes like big blue marbles over the white mask covering the lower half of his face.

'It's all there', she'll reply, 'Six big black sacks of screaming matches, two bags full of yessirs, nosirs, six bags fullsirs', all neatly tied with sticky tape and all stickered. One stack alone crammed with curses she can't bear to think of, especially the C word. And what of the bags full of silences, bloated like helium balloons? Jim could put a clamp on his mouth for days. Brooding days. Up late, then off out. Not that he was a big boozer, 'It passes the hours'. She'd stopped trying to pin down an exact time for his return. All those twenty minutes past maybe or ten minutes past 'When I fucking feel like it', could go in the transit van as well.

Ann imagines Mr Transit Van Man smiling under his mask. Why wouldn't he? Isn't he in a good job and getting well paid for it? Still, it's not a job Ann would choose herself. She'd heard on the radio of a woman who chloroformed kittens and put them in a biscuit tin and then, what did the woman do? Shove them under the bed and forget about them. She shivers although the shopping centre is warm as a furnace. Tom Jones singing *Sex Bomb* explodes from the ceiling, competing with a wail of heavy metal from Virgin Records nearby.

A neighbour across the road from her thinks he's Elvis. He has a karaoke machine and sings out onto the street, standing in the window with the microphone as if facing a packed concert hall. It annoys the hell out of her. Months ago she'd gotten up the courage and gone across the road in her dressing gown and slippers.

'Don't go making a show of us', Jim said, 'You know that fucking shower are pig ignorant'.

Standing under their porch light, she felt very small and very vulnerable. Above her head in his box room, *Suspicious Minds*, was being belted out by the man who thinks he's Elvis. She braced herself and knocked twice with her knuckles. Nancy came to the door, a tiny woman with an aggressive tilt to her head and a gleam in her eye.

'Please, would you mind asking himself to turn down the volume a bit?' Ann said. Nancy nodded and grunted something that Ann took to be a grudging okay. And for the rest of that week, two years ago now, it was.

Sausages. There'd be sausages again today for dinner. If she could string all the sausages they've eaten at the kitchen table in the last decade even, there'd be enough to circle the planet. Sausages with herbs and stuffing and then there are the ones with no meat. 'What good is a sausage without meat?' Jim said, the one and only time she produced them. Followed by a string of swear words of course. Ann had tossed that string of curses onto the pan and burnt them to a crisp with the black pudding that she bought by the ring in the butcher shop. The look on Jim's face of sheer stupid confusion made her laugh despite the fact that she hated him only two minutes before that and would have stabbed him with the kitchen knife if a sausage hadn't burst and spit grease right up into her face.

Looking for a job? There's always a couple of those. Looking for a job little slips of paper. Are you looking for a job? I mean you, you there? Like a wanted ad for the army. 'You mean … me?' Then, as if from nowhere, she could hear Jim doing his phoney take off of John Wayne. Jim loves cowboy pictures. 'They don't show 'em like that anymore', he says if there's a cowboy film on the telly. He loves all the cowboy films but John Wayne gives him the biggest kick of all. 'Are you lookin' for a job … are you lookin' … at me? Like hell I'm lookin' for a job, like fucking hell I am'.

'Give me a break', Jim says if Ann broaches the question of looking for work. It does her head in to see him in his vest at the table. And noon is early. Un-shaven, un-washed, his hair like a wire brush. Tapping at an egg as if trying to detonate a bomb. Being made redundant was the worst thing to happen to him. Only forty when the axe fell. A cigarette factory too so not much sympathy there. Still, it isn't Jim who's responsible for poisoning the country. And the queues in the labour exchange were still growing. Pity there wasn't anyone in the queue before her with Nancy and Elvis. None of the other neighbours seemed to mind. On the third trip across the road to the Cabaret Venue as Jim calls it, Nancy came to the door, hostility written all over her face.

'Go and shite', she said before Ann could get a word out. Ann stammered in confusion something to the effect of: 'Well, I know we all like a bit of enjoyment at the end of the day but …'

Nancy twisted her mouth as if changing gear in the red mini parked outside the gate and didn't let Ann finish the sentence.

'You'd know all about having a bit of enjoyment, isn't that right?' she said, her eyes like coals in the dark. 'Better than Dr Quirkey's you are, sure everyone knows that'.

'Ha! I told you so', Jim said when Ann, white-faced, came back across the road, leaving out the bit about herself and the reference to Dr Quirkey's Good Time Emporium.

'That shower are as ignorant as my arse, now leave it. We'll just turn up the volume here instead and then you won't hear him'. Which he did. Ann thought her head would burst and when she went upstairs she got into bed and covered her head, but she could still hear Elvis, and worse, the sound of the television coming up the stairs, very loud and very clear. Better than Quirkey's? Is that how they saw her? In the same light as a place she wouldn't be seen dead in, all slot machines and flashing lights.

Do you have a drink problem? That one's always in extra big bold letters. As if the drinkers with the drink problems have eyesight trouble too. *Please don't feed the Guide Dog if he's on duty.* Whoever put that one there had a sense of humour. At least the guide dog is fucking working as Jim might say. *Flat to let*. A right little earner that. The fact they do indeed have a spare room gives Ann little comfort. Five years ago now and not one word from Paulie their only son. The week before, coming from the city on the Luas, she'd seen a young chap the spit and image of him. Jesus, how her heart pounded. The young chap had the same slim body and the very same face, except his hair was a lighter colour. But it had been five years and she thought maybe he'd changed his hair or something. But then the young chap on the Luas opened his mouth and what came out? Not 'Howya Ma', or 'Great to see you and sure everyone deserves a good time Ma', but a load of gibberish, at least that's how it sounded to Ann. Polish or German or something like that.

Air Ticket, One Way to Paris jumps out among the slips for second-hand cars or morning classes. Not that she'd be going to Paris. Or morning classes either. It's ages since herself and Jim have gone anywhere nice. The summer before, in a rare burst of nostalgia, they went back to the house where Jim's mother had lived, right up until her death. A right Tartar that one had been too she remembers – though Jim has placed her on a pedestal.

'Fucking Corporation', he muttered when he saw the steel gates around the site. It was a Sunday so no workers around to stop them squeezing through a gap. They knew they were trespassing but Jim was adamant. All the back of the house was open and they could still see the scraps of wallpaper and the old fireplace like a big open wound festering. Ann noticed a dead bird, a swallow she thought, on the floor beside the stairs that led up from the kitchen into the bedroom. She could feel her stomach churning. The tiny body was smashed open. Worst of all she could hear the baby birds cheeping in the roof.

'Must be a nest up there', she said to Jim, indicating the roof, 'She must have dashed herself off the lintel flying up'.

'They won't last too long now', is all he said. 'Come on, let's get out of this fucking place'. He was upset for the whole of that day but said nothing more about it, smothering the house in silence. Paulie hadn't taken it from the ground.

Paulie. Only ten when it happened. When he was left stood in the garden at twenty past three of an afternoon with no-one in the house to answer his knock. Ann can still hardly bear to think of it. And all that madness for a good time with a man she barely knew and who wouldn't give her the time of day if he passed her in the street tomorrow. As if in slow motion, she sees herself flying out of the house that Wednesday at noon, the car's engine running, a case in her hand, crammed with her best gear. She'd gotten her hair done professionally, had highlights put in and she's wearing good perfume … She barely makes out the face leaning towards her as she opens the door and scoots into the front seat. 'Like Bonnie and fucking Clyde', Jim said after the madness cooled down and she came home. For two weeks she had stayed away with a man she flirted with at the betting office where she worked, a 'fucking punter' Jim said, 'Why the fuck couldn't you have gone for the boss at least'. As soon as he could, Paulie had left and not one word since.

Some of the notices it seems to her are never taken down. The one for *Christian Choir needs new members* has been there for weeks. Maybe Elvis will join and then there'd be no need for him to stand in his box-room window with a karaoke microphone in his hand. Ann catches sight of her face in a square of glass that has no notice on it, a blank space. She sees the lines near her eyes and the furrows at each corner of her mouth. She looks like an ad herself. An ad someone's put in looking to be cheered up, someone in need of a good time.

FUCHSIA

Cian hears Una open and close the drawers of the dressing table.

'Don't go yet, the night's still young', he says through a half yawn, reaching out, pulling her back to bed, wrapping her in the scent of his skin and half sleep. But she withdraws from his arms and he lets her slide away. He knows her mind is already leaving this room with its one small window.

'I'll bring you a brew', she says, surprising him instead. His heart swells with happiness, his mouth widening into a smile. There's nothing he wouldn't do for her and he would have her all to himself for a whole week.

'I'll make lunch, or we can eat at that hotel down by the lake if you'd prefer', he says.

'Okay, I'll take a look while I'm out; you can never be sure with these places'. When she leaves the room, he moves to her side of the bed but can find no trace of her. The bed feels cold, the mattress harder. Una's left the bedside light on and it throws shadows across pale green walls. It's only 7am. On an ordinary morning he'd be shuffling under the bedclothes and grabbing an extra five minutes before heading to work. He certainly won't miss driving in traffic for the next few days.

Stretching his legs, extending his feet, he feels his muscles easing out. His thoughts drift over the car ride down from the city the day before, the string of country towns, each one similar to the next. The same air of neglect straggled out of broken chimney pots, webbed in the spidery panes of cracked glass in derelict buildings on the edges of the towns. Although early afternoon, clusters of men mostly were loitering outside doorways of public houses; smoking cigarettes, their faces ashen, desolate; eyes fixed on a far off place.

Una scalds the pot, swirling the water around the bottom three times in an anti-clockwise direction, using real tea-leaves. The radio is a low hum. Above the kitchen sink the window frame is leafed in fuchsia, ripe berries splay across the glass. She once had a shade of lipstick like it when she was much younger, a shade she wouldn't dare to wear now. She tries to remember the name. *Midnight Rose* or *Crimson Morning*? Something frivolous. Fuchsia grows wild around the landscape. Its vibrant colour seems insistent, sneaking its way over walls and hedges, creeping around whitewashed gables. Sometimes, it catches her unawares when she looks out the cottage windows. Setting the pot down on a tray to brew, she makes toast for Cian. She spreads butter then hears a whirr of wing circle her head from the butterfly that rushed in the door of the cottage on their arrival. 'A good omen', Cian said with a note of optimism she really wished she could share.

Una notices the pair of bright orange wings hover over the curtain rail before darting across the room in search of an exit point. She puts down the knife, rubs her hands across her wide hips and opens the back door to see if it'll fly out.

'Stupid butterfly', she mutters under her breath, watching it spin past the entrance a few times, surfing the air before eventually breaking free over a hedge bleeding with fuchsia. The smell of mint in the herb garden near the door rises towards her, its delicate stems quivering in the breeze. She closes another button on her cardigan, glad she's packed her heavy winter coat.

The next morning Una finds herself doing the same as the day before, only this time Cian doesn't try to draw her back to him and when she takes in the tray he has fallen asleep. They'd stayed up really late the night before so they could see the constellations of stars in the night sky.

'Imagine', he'd said, 'All this brightness wiped out at home with so many streetlights and here, crystal clear'. There was awe and reverence in his tone, like a child discovering the world for the first time. Looking up at a crazy number of stars sieving through the sky, Una felt very small. Late October chill drove her inside a couple of times to warm beside the stove.

'I don't think I could ever tire of such a sight', he said when he finally came in, blowing breath onto his mottled hands. He seemed taller, lit up in himself. 'Damn streetlights. It's worth the trip to see the stars properly', he said, bending his tall frame and taking out of the cardboard box stowed beside the vegetable rack the half bottle of the *Jameson* they'd bought in one of the towns . She'd shook her head; the whiskey would keep her from the sleep she craved, whereas on him it usually had the opposite effect.

'If we had cloves, I could rustle up a hot whiskey', he joked.

'No need to go overboard', she said, her tone sharper than intended. She touched his arm as she passed by him then took out a tin of cocoa from the supply box, prising the lid open with the end of a fork. The rich exotic fragrance of the thick powdery substance engulfed her. For a moment she felt a little dizzy. But the moment passed. Cian just had the one whiskey, tossing it back quickly and shuddering as it went down.

'I don't know why you drink it', she said, 'Obviously, it's a chore'.

Cian said nothing. The truth was, the whiskey had hit the spot and was followed by a rush of affection for his wife. When she laid her mug on the table he moved to take her in his arms. But he felt her back shrivel away from him and she would not turn her head to receive his kiss.

'I'm tired, so are you', she said and he left it at that. When she eventually came to bed it was enough that she snuggled into his warmth before falling asleep.

And now, as the birds are calling and the dawn rinses over the roads and surrounding hills, Cian wakes and sees the tray of toast grown cold, a skim already forming on the tea. There's a slight sourness in his mouth, the aftermath of the nightcap, but not enough to give him a hangover. He hears Una moving about in the hallway. The lightness of her step is replaced by the sound of stamping shoes, ridding them of leaves that are now dry enough to shake free. He closes his eyes, briefly imagining them back in the heat of two summers ago in Madrid, a carafe of wine on the table, the air throbbing with the insistent beat of flamenco dancers.

Unaware that Cian is awake and listening to the sounds of her stamping feet, Una looks at yesterday's leaves and wet gravel on the floor tiles. Smaller leaves are like tiny hands, bigger sized ones are just beginning to curl inward, their veiny undersides a gnarled, off-white colour. As soon as she comes back from her walk she'll sweep them up into a neat pile and scatter them in the garden so they go back into the soil. Outside, the same burnished leaves clog the guttering and nestle into hollows in the pathway that leads from the cottage down to the lake shore. The walk is long enough to make her feel she has gotten some exercise yet short enough that she doesn't tire. Spits of rain prickle her face so she turns up the hood of her blue woollen coat and wraps her long white scarf around her neck. In the last two days she has not met a soul walking on this road even though there's a steady stream of traffic driving towards the nearest town. The other cottages she passes are beginning to show signs of life; plumes of smoke spiral from chimneys. The walls of the cottages are hung with the straggly remains of summer baskets with barely a glimpse of their former glory. She tries to imagine how they must look with the sun shining, their colours blazing against whitewashed walls. Beyond the gardens light gleams in the windows, the early morning rituals already begun of calling children from their beds, shaving or boiling an egg or indeed, stoking up a contrary stove. Frenzied barking announces her approach but the dogs are all secured behind gates or locked up in sheds. Una thinks of Margaret calling little Liam from his bed, making sure he's up in plenty of time for school, that he has time for a square meal. The moon and the streetlights will still be switched on, the two rows of houses in various stages of undress. The heron that is now a familiar sight on the rooftops will be stood with his head resting on his chest. Offering false promises. Una shoves her hands deeper into her coat pockets.

'What a ginormous bird Mam', Liam said, months ago now, the first time he saw a heron appear on the apex of their garden shed. 'Bet it's a stork!'

'No pet, although his wings are wide enough to fly around the world and his bill strong enough to hold the weight of a precious bundle, it's a heron, not a stork'.

'He's a magic bird; he can turn himself into whatever he wants'. Liam was so insistent that eventually she said, 'Of course he can and who knows, maybe he will'. Mother and son smiled at each other. When they looked out the window again the blue hued heron was gone.

Una shakes away the memory and wraps her scarf tighter. Her thoughts linger on her sister Margaret. Ten years older and with two grown up children.

'Plenty of time on her hands', Cian often says, leaving the phrase 'busybody' hanging in the air. But she was glad of her help these last months.

A few yards ahead, Una sees a dim glow behind the mullioned glass of the hotel perched near the winding path that joins the road with the shore. Breakfast begins early in the dining room. It's written on a sign over the brown mahogany reception desk, placed next to the copper bell she'd rung the day before. There'd been no-one at reception and through an open door behind the desk herself and Cian glimpsed the kitchen staff scurrying by wearing blue stripped chequered aprons and white hats. Music drifted around the lobby area, gliding over the dusty tops of picture rails, settling on faded antimacassars shawled over armchairs ranged around the large bay window facing onto the lake view. Smells of bacon and cabbage wafted out also, and another smell, soup mixed with custard, it was hard to tell. The receptionist shot down the adjoining stairwell, her face rosy with exertion. Just before she came within earshot, Cian looked at Una, his left eyebrow raised in the way she'd always found attractive and said:

'We can try somewhere else, we've got all day'.

'No, here's fine. Besides, I'm quite hungry', she'd said, and was pleasantly surprised to realise that she was.

On Wednesday, there's still a spill of fuchsia against the windows of the cottage. Today, the colour seems full of rage however, as if leaking its anger through the glass. Pearls of rain cling to its silky petals. She hears the bath running, can picture Cian testing the water cautiously with his foot before stepping in, his body lean and supple. Today they are going to explore the nearest big town. The forecast is for moderate winds and small showers. She drifts into the sitting room, its north facing aspect making it a little darker than the other rooms in the cottage but there's lots of cosy lamps and some candles. Perhaps they'll light them later on. She rakes the fire and finds a still warm centre. No need to clean the grate, it would be good for another day or two.

'A fire will make all the difference in this room', Cian said the first evening, 'It will help to clear that musty smell. We'll need to know the weather forecasts too', he added as an afterthought.

Apart from squalls of rain, so far there'd been no gales or gusts, no need for them to watch the weather anxiously. Through the open door of the sitting room, she hears Cian humming in the bath, probably floating under the expensive bath suds she's brought, his eyes closed, his dark hair just tipping the water, his long legs bent at the knees, almost in the birthing position. She feels a shock go through her and for a moment steadies herself. She finds her way to the hall, puts on her outdoor shoes, coat and scarf and calls a low good bye to him before she closes the door.

The next morning Una again wakes early but too early to rise or drink coffee. Wild birds are anxiously calling to each other and when those sounds settle down she hears the thermostat of the boiler clicking in. She pulls the covers around her shoulders, listening to Cian's even breathing. The outing to the nearest town the day before had put him in such high spirits at the outset, attentive to her every need, insisting she buy something expensive in the handbag shop in the small shopping centre.

'I've more handbags than I know what to do with', she'd replied but to please him she bought a clutch bag, the cheapest she could find. She barely touched her food in an Italian restaurant. 'Are you okay?' Cian asked when she again only picked at the fruit salad, one of her favourite desserts.

'I'm fine, I'll eat later. We'll bring home crusty bread and make some soup', she said. He nodded but his expression lost some of its sheen and when he paid the bill he was not as generous with the tip as he might otherwise have been.

She tries to concentrate on the telephone call she'll make to her sister later on in the morning. Making small talk, asking if everything is okay, if Liam is behaving and telling her when to expect their return. Around eleven would be good to make the call. Margaret would have the house shining by then, all the cups and plates and knives and forks and spoons dried and put away in their individual compartments in the cutlery drawer, the shopping packed away, the labels on the tins and jars facing out, the lunch settings placed neatly on the table.

The lake surface looks cross, rolling and folding, roiling against the rim of the shore. A dog and a young woman come down from the houses nearby. She's seen them before, the black and white mongrel, running to the edge of the water and running back again, watching for the signal from its owner who throws the ball that will be brought back like a boomerang, every single time. Una guesses that no matter how often that ball will be thrown, the dog will retrieve it. The young woman waves to her and shouts something but the wind is too strong and Una doesn't hear what was said. She returns the wave and makes her way back to the cottage.

'We might try that hotel again', Cian suggests later on, 'It's not too bad, is it?'

'It's fine', she replies. But she would prefer to go somewhere else, a big hotel with plush carpets and long, gleaming mirrors. Where the waitresses are dressed in smart black uniforms, starched white blouses and wearing dark stockings and good, leather shoes. Anywhere but the hotel on the strand, the notices advertising bingo sessions and visiting musicians months out of date still covering the hall stand, the smell of cabbage drifting its sour perfume over the faded wallpaper, the heaviness of the dark furniture.

'We can leave our coats in the car', Una says, when they arrive into the car park. 'I doubt anyone will make off with them'.

Inside the hotel, although a fire is lit in the lobby, Una can still detect the faint smell of damp. They go straight into the dining room and choose a table for two by the window.

'Will you have a starter?' he asks, rubbing his hands together. His face has colour in it, his eyes are bright.

'No, I'll have dessert instead', she says. His hands brush hers briefly before he busies himself going over the menu. Una tries not to stare at the other occupants of the dining room, elderly couples taking advantage of out of season prices.

'The blue rinse brigade', he whispers to her, catching her mood. 'Bet they got their week for a song'.

'Are you ready to order?' the waitress asks, pen and notebook poised, directing her question towards Cian.

'Beef with mixed vegetables', Una says. The waitress doesn't miss a beat but writes it down and swiftly turns on her heel. There's a faint greasy feel to the plastic covering the menu. Una rubs her hands in the white paper napkin on the table and reaches for the jug of water bobbing with ice-cubes and a tired slice of lemon. When the meal comes, she barely makes a dent in the thick slices of meat and the mound of mashed potatoes dripping with thick gravy.

'Ready to go home?' Cian asks her the next day.

'I guess'. She busies herself cleaning down the sink and neatly tying up the rubbish bags. She doesn't want the next occupants to think badly of them.

'I think we're leaving this place cleaner than we found it', he says, taking his tea and going outside to sit near the back door. The air is damp. He checks the bench but it's under shelter and miraculously, has escaped the worst of the night's downpour. No matter how hard he's offered to help she's refused, saying, 'You know I'll only be going around after you'. However, she asked him to clean the grate and empty the ashes into the large tin barrel in one of the outhouses. Now he feels curiously tired, despite having slept so well for the week. Perhaps it's true what people say about not realising how exhausted you are until you get the chance to rest. And it was good to be near the lake although the few times he'd walked the shore with Una she'd seemed distracted.

'This is better than the mountains', he'd said to her more than once, picking up a pebble and skimming it over the waves, 'You can breathe here'.

The day before, he'd driven down to the shore himself. Una's tiredness had forced her to bed in late afternoon. The shore was empty, nothing but pebbles and sand and some high grass and stones fringed by trees craning towards the sky. Across the lake he could see hills undulating upwards, dotted with sheep and wisps of smoke streaking across the landscape. He turned up the collar of his coat, the wind was wrinkling the lake water, driving it towards him. He left the pebbly shore and wandered through the trees, seeing the usual black rings in clearings where summer fires had been lit a few short months before. There was also the usual assortment of empty beer cans and cigarette butts. Further on he looked down and saw a child's summer sandal, abandoned, lost. Possibly searched for by a parent on the shore, carried up here by a dog or perhaps lost here where he'd found it. The sandal was a bright colour and he guessed would fit a child of two or three years old. He felt the breath go out of him, his shoulders sagged in on himself and he leaned against a sturdy oak. When tears came he let them roll unchecked down his face. He stood there a long time before picking up the little shoe and burying it further back in grass that seemed taller and greener.

Last night was the first time in months they'd made love. Curiously, it had been Una who made the first tentative movements. He was scared to respond in case it wasn't what she wanted. He had misread her body before. But there were signs of a softening in her earlier on in the evening. They'd listened to the radio for a while. The afternoon's rest had done her good. Her face was brighter and she'd smiled at him when she looked up and caught him staring at her. He'd been content to sit in the cosy glow of the fire, while the radio played and outside the wind whipped around the gable.

'Remember the winter it snowed and we couldn't go anywhere for days?' she said after a while, turning off the radio and coming to sit nearer to him. Logs that burned all through the evening collapsed softly into glowing embers.

'You said we would run out of words quicker than milk and bread, isn't that so?' he reminded her, brushing back a stray wisp of her hair.

'Yes. I remember', she said. 'But we didn't. Once we had each other, we got through it'. Later, there'd been no mistaking the way her hands moved over his body. It was as if the long absence of her scent, her mouth and her rhythms had never happened.

He swirls the dregs of the tea into the mint garden. When he looks up he can see Una's small dark head pass behind the window. Her hair pulled back in a ponytail makes her appear even younger than she is. She pauses for a moment, her expression tense as if she is trying to remember something. Just as suddenly her features relax and she waves to him, her pale face framed in fuchsia.

LIFE AFTER BENNIE

Barely 6.30 am but already the bedroom is flooded with light. Taking down the black-out curtains was one of the first things Jake insisted on when Bennie was finally installed in the nursery. It seemed a good idea at the time, liberating. Now he's not so sure.

On weekdays it's Ruby who's first out of bed, pushing her feet into slippers, fastening the belt on her faded green dressing gown. Weekends, it's his turn. That's the deal. Ruby does the weekday shifts, weekends are his call. But this morning he's surprised by a silence that's welcome if unexpected.

Ruby turns towards him, twisting the sheet away from her bare shoulder, her dark hair fanning out over the pillow.

'I'm moulting', she's been saying lately, especially after brushing, alarmed at the amount of loose hairs that flutter onto their wooden floors or clog up her brush.

'Don't worry', the doctor said, 'Very normal after having a baby and to be expected. It'll soon right itself'.

'All very well for him', Ruby says. He's not the one who'll end up looking like a bald eagle. Ruby's hair has always been her best feature, thick and lustrous at its best. They both know it's highly unlikely her hair loss will be that severe but it's got to the stage where they don't joke about it anymore.

Jake looks down at his sleeping wife, tempted to touch her. Before Bennie came along he'd have stroked Ruby's skin, woken her with a caress of his lips on her pale translucent eyelids. She'd kiss him back and say, 'Your stubble's like sandpaper, go shave'. But not really meaning it, because that first time he was about to do just that ... when he wasn't sure if she did mean it ... she'd pulled him back to bed and said 'Okay Scratchy, I'm all yours'.

He sees the faint weave of veins pulsing at her throat and the shadows under the sweep of her lashes. More evidence of life after-Bennie. As soon as the thought comes, guilt quickly follows. Still ... barely 6.30am and already Jake's waiting for the signal to strike up yet another exhausting round. Nappies, bottles and gobbledegook.

It seems forever ago since those carefree weekends when they first moved in together. Late nights in Temple Bar followed by mornings in bed then off to town for afternoon coffee with friends. Or long, lingering afternoons in Dun Laoghaire or Bray, strolling the pier, doused in the scent of seaweed and fish and chips.

It's been a while also since they'd had friends around. Jake misses the sound of cars pulling up outside their house, laughter floating up the path, then good food, great music and soft candlelight melting down the hours.

'Who can blame them?' he says whenever Ruby remarks, 'Looks like the world is passing us by'.

Of course he doesn't say so but Jake blames the visitor fall-off to Bennie's colic, which kicked in big time soon after he came home from hospital. Come to think of it, Bennie seemed to be the only 'unsettled' baby in the ward, heard quarter ways down the corridor at visiting times. How could a tiny baby cry so loudly and so long?

Jake leaves his side of the bed, deciding it's always better to be one step ahead of the posse. He's careful however, not to disturb Ruby. She needed all the rest she could get. Even if Bennie is sleeping better these last weeks, they can take nothing for granted. It's not long since the last bout of colic had him in its grip and they've both been holding their breaths since.

Downstairs, Jake decides to make coffee, if he's lucky he'll get a chance to drink it while it's hot. On the worktop in the red and white tiled kitchen, the special bottles to minimise wind are sterilised and filled with boiled, cooled water and lined up like soldiers. Ruby's last act before she came to bed the night before, refusing the offer of a glass of wine when Bennie finally fell asleep. 'You know one leads to two and I don't want a thick head in the morning', was her swift yet decisive reply.

Jake's thoughts again turn to the doctor recently telling them; 'Your son's colic seems to have run its course'. He's the same doctor who told Ruby her hair loss is nothing to worry about. Yet the plughole in the shower still clogs up with what looks like big fur balls.

'What if the colic re-occurs?' Ruby persisted, her brow creased with lines, making her look older than her early thirties. 'Sometimes his face scrunches up, as if he's waiting for it to happen', she explained to the doctor, but again, she was assured there was nothing to worry about.

'You've been lucky; Bennie's colic could have lasted much longer. For all we know, he might still be anticipating a spasm', the doctor said, 'He'll soon learn that his symptoms have disappeared'. He closed Benny's file, an act that signalled the end of the visit.

'Is it possible that Bennie remembers the pain and is bracing himself for it?' Ruby said to Jake the minute they were outside the clinic. Even thinking about the way Bennie's legs would bend towards his stomach and his tiny hands curl into fists in an agony of pain made her grip the buggy handle until the bones beneath her knuckles showed through.

'His memory isn't like a photograph with a negative on standby', Jake said quickly. Yet, for Ruby the worry seed was planted.

In fact, Jake's noticed how she worries over lots of things. She doesn't like opening the window in Bennie's room for starters. In case bugs get in. 'It'd be just our luck he'd get a bite from a rare insect', she says whenever Jake suggests leaving it open an inch or so. And there's no blankets, no Siree. Bennie sleeps in a little zip up cotton bag that leaves his arms free so at least there's no danger he'll be tangled up in bedclothes. Jake wouldn't mind being upstairs, tangled up in bedclothes with Ruby but that was wishful thinking, definitely.

Instead, he's downstairs on a Saturday morning at an unearthly hour, spooning instant into a cup. Soon, the early train into the city will be heard crossing over the track nearby, starting slow, then gathering momentum, like one of Ruby's contractions he sometimes thinks. Bennie coming into their world certainly changed it. But the trains were still the same even if life for himself and Ruby wasn't. When they first moved into the estate, Ruby loved the rhythmic sound of the train engines and the proximity to the station was a selling point advantage as far as she was concerned.

'It's so romantic, all those strangers waiting on platforms', she'd said, 'Who knows what journeys they're planning, places to go, people to meet'.

'Hardly the Orient Express, 'Jake said, always the practical one. 'Places to go, people to meet! Heading to work most like'. The truth of the matter now though is he's very glad of the station, as the second car has had to be sold. Ruby's romantic notions have also suffered cutbacks. Gradually, as Bennie's screaming wore down the hours and tore out her heart, she began to resent the rumbling sounds of each passing train.

'Will it never stop', she'd say when Bennie was at his worst. Her nerves were so finely turned; she appeared to hear everything amplified. And worst of all, their savings were dwindling.

Jake wonders if Ruby will ever go back to work after extending her maternity leave, without pay. Or indeed if there will be a job to go back to. Even at that, she doesn't want to tempt fate by making plans. It's still early days since Bennie's last episode.

'I can't leave him now, what if the pain comes back and I'm not with him? I'd never forgive myself', she says if Jake even mentions a returning to work scenario.

'Any coffee going?' Her voice startles him into the present and he swings around. 'Yeah, have this one', he says, handing her the mug, adding, 'You should have stayed in bed longer'. She takes it from him and even though it's summer, her fingers brushing his are cold to the touch. It's the routine, can't seem to escape it', she says, matter-of-factly. 'I've checked on Benny, he's good for about five minutes. Just about long enough to get this down'. She grimaces as the hot liquid floods her mouth. She reaches for the milk jug and pours in more, adding one extra sugar. He notices that her shoulders seem permanently hunched. He wants to reach out and rub her neck, ease out the knots of stress held in her body. But he stays where he is. Their kitchen window faces onto a large field. The yellow metal crane is long gone; and with it the promise of a small shopping centre, crèche and community centre. Now, it's just a field, blazing with wild poppies and strewn with paper bags flapping like grounded birds.

Bennie's first cry of the day startles Ruby into action.

'Finish your coffee, I'll go', Jake insists, 'The kettle's boiled, it won't take a minute to heat up his bottle'.

'It's fine, I'm nearly done', Ruby says, taking a final gulp and swallowing without seeming to taste. That's another thing Jake is beginning to resent, how quickly meals are eaten, everything rushed through.

Ruby clatters up the stairs, calling to their son in an octave higher than her usual tone. Jake looks out the window, his gaze held by swallows, feeding on the wing above the overgrown, derelict grounds. Swallows flitted through the doorway, flying over himself and Ruby in the tiny Church in Kinsale where they'd gotten married the summer before, their baby son already breathing in Ruby's womb.

'Just imagine, those birds fly so many thousands of miles', Ruby said to him afterwards at the reception, 'It could be as far away as the moon', she'd added dreamily.

'A lot of them don't make it', he'd replied, then seeing her crestfallen expression he'd raised his glass of champagne, clinked it to hers and said, 'Here's to swallows, long may they make it to wherever that happens to be'.

Jake removes the cling-film covering Bennie's porridge powder. It's ready to be mixed with some of the formula which he now measures into one of the bottles, shaking it until the powder is completely dissolved. The first train of the day, heard as a low grumbling sound, gathers momentum as it passes on the track nearby. Again, Jake remembers Ruby's tense face, the sleepless nights and the pacing up and down. He shakes the bottle even harder. So hard that it makes a loud swishing noise and threatens to burst through the lid. The breath goes out of him. By the time Ruby comes back into the kitchen with Bennie in her arms, he has regained most of his composure.

Jake gives her the bottle for their son, his hands still shaking a little but if Ruby notices she doesn't comment. She settles at the table and smoothes back Bennie's damp hair as he drinks.

'The swallows are out there having a ball', he says at last.

'It's still hard to imagine the distance they've come, they must keep the negative of their journey as well as the photograph', Ruby replies, hunching her shoulders even tighter, adding as an afterthought,

'And a lot of them don't make it at that'.

'But a lot of them do', Jake says, trying hard to be optimistic. He looks at Ruby over the blonde head of their son, wanting her to cut him some slack. But her eyes have a blank expression and the space between them could be as far away as the moon.

ANTS

Everywhere they were. Black crawling dots, pinpricks of jet scurrying over her white worktops. The cutlery drawer is packed full with them, squished under knives, sliding down spoons. They breathe out shapes in the walls, bulge under the lino. Tiny black shadows dart like minnows underneath the cooker, under cups and plates, slithering along the cat's dish by the back door. In the beginning, Frank told her to get rid of the cat, that it must be the cat's food attracts them in.

'Must be', he said, 'Why else would they be here?'

Before that conclusion however, he accused her of being paranoid, multiplying a stray ant or two, magnifying them into plague proportions. The latest now is that he's convinced everyone has them, a seasonal thing. As if somehow that makes it alright.

Sometimes he calls her 'Sugar-bun', his pet name but today she's just plain Cora with no frills. She feels plain too. Pale and worn like her faded blue dressing gown. Frank has already left the problem of the ants behind.

Moved three steps ahead into morning traffic lanes. Then he'll breeze into the office with his big, cheeky grin, be handed his breakfast. Hot toast smothered in butter probably. Handed to him by a smiling secretary, her mouth smothered in lipstick. Cora wonders if Frank calls her 'Sugar-bun' also.

Maybe she is paranoid, afraid to look inside her toaster, worried in case she'll find a hive in there, a honeycomb of ants. They remind her of bees, always buzzing around, always on the move. Hadn't they somehow infiltrated her walls, her bricks and mortar? It makes her skin crawl. She counted eight that morning swarming on a cup. Eight fat ants. Fuckers. Swear words come easily to Cora when she's frustrated. Or angry. Swear words crawling around her head. She'd thrown the cup straight into the bin which still left eight black bodies to crush under her thumb. Alice, her only child, had tried to make light of the ant thing. At first.

'They're like jam', she said, 'Like blackberry jam Mum'.

Cora thought it strange that her only child would think the black gunge of squashed ants under her mother's thumb reminded her of jam. Those slathers of summer tastes spread between slices of white bread. Fresh, delicious, mouth watering. Summer tastes and sounds. Alice and Frank playing hide and go seek, laughter tickling over Cora's skin as she lay in the soft grass of summer meadows.

'Or caviar', Alice said another time, trying hard to smile.

This morning, when Alice comes down for her breakfast, there's a guarded look in her eyes. Bowls are carefully scrutinized before cereal is poured out. Alice half expects an avalanche to tumble out with the cornflakes, an avalanche of ants doing somersaults before landing with a big plop into the warm milk. She hates the tight look on her mother's face. It was there too a few months earlier when she came home from school with head lice. Cora almost had a stroke. All those hours of fine combing and shampooing before Alice was finally given a clean bill of health. Her scalp had been scrubbed raw.

'Of course, your father can jeer', Cora said, 'He's not the one has to do it. Oh no, he's not the one picking out dead bodies from his only child's head'.

The smell of the shampoo had also sickened both of them. And for weeks after, Cora insisted on Alice's hair being scraped back from her forehead, a style Alice hates.

Alice barely touches her cereal. Instead, she gulps her tea and grabs her schoolbag. A whirlwind of blue uniform and she's out the door before Cora can say anything.

Out of the corner of her eye, Cora spots it, trekking purposefully from behind the fridge. Christ, now they were invading the other side of the kitchen. Maybe the cat food is attracting them after all. Frank said the cat should be gotten rid of. The ants get the scent of the food and then they're in, like Flynn. She hadn't laughed at his feeble joke. What did he care? Off to the office, an aftershave gleam on his face, his briefcase held like a trophy in his hand. Promotion certainly did no harm as far as housekeeping money was concerned but he was scarcely ever at home. There were always those meetings, networking sessions as he called them.

'Absolutely essential Sugar-bun, that's how business gets done'.

Cora has tried poison. Her local hardware store is full of these slim red containers, shelf loads of powders and sprays. Two weeks ago now she'd gotten into her car and drove to the shopping centre. She played with the idea of going out of the area but the effort seemed too much. She bought the shampoo for the lice in the supermarket two estates from her own. At the time she'd felt so miserable she couldn't face anyone she knew. Especially the Lollipop

Lady at the traffic lights who always gave her a big wave with her oversized white lollipop.

But two weeks ago she decided that the local hardware would be okay. Besides, ants didn't appear to be as bad as lice which seemed to imply that Alice and herself for that matter, were dirty, unclean in some way.

'Of course, you know they only go for clean hair', the chemist said, noticing Cora's agitation. 'It's just bad luck your daughter got them. A bit of vigilance and this', she added, holding up an aerosol, 'will soon do the trick'.

It hadn't been as easy as that though. It had taken quite a few doses and quite an amount of vigilance before Alice got the all clear. Finally. Cora felt like a sniper going through Alice's long, brown hair, picking off dead lice, watching for any new eggs which might hatch. Then, the fine combing, the lice like black dots on the white comb. Like black lies on a white page.

In the hardware, Declan the hardware man was equally as optimistic as the chemist had been. 'This'll do it Missus. This'll get the bastards'. He looked at her with a huge grin of satisfaction. She wondered did he have ants then decided no; his house was probably ant free. He looked far too smug to have anything crawling around his house. His hardware shop seemed to be thoroughly organised, everything in its place right down to the thick yard brushes propped beside the counter. Brushes thick as Frank's bristle in the mornings, a bristle that he lathers with Calvin Klein shaving foam and then caresses with the blade. Frank had to have scalding hot water first thing, no matter if the sky fell or the world collapsed in on itself like a giant soufflé. He doesn't care so much if there's no kettle boiled for tea or no toast made but the bathroom must be kept free. The hot water is on a timer and he has first call. When he makes his first big deal, 'We'll be outta' here' he sometimes says in a big fake American accent. Easy for him. She's the one burning with shame in the local hardware shop. A house full of ants. And poor Alice that time with the head lice. Cora was the one stood in the chemist shop asking for some foul smelling shampoo. All that combing and watching for signs of movement in Alice's beautiful brown hair. It was definitely her best feature, inherited from Frank's side. Cora's hair was thin and lank. Maybe she should go to the hairdresser's more often. The pampering of the hairdresser's hands massaging her scalp was gentle, unhurried, the way lovemaking with Frank used to be. The way she'd be asked whether this was alright or that was okay or would she like to try a new style or a new colour? Then, relaxing into the music playing in the salon. Silky music for women who were getting their hair done for a night out or for a special occasion.

'What does himself think of the ants?' Declan asked her while she stood there, her face burning with shame.

'What does he make of the bastards?' He sucked in his breath through his teeth, obviously delighted to be discussing Cora's infestation, secure that his own house is ant free. As if Declan cared. Cora couldn't really expect him to care though, in fairness. After all, what was it to him if she was found half eaten to death by a squad of ants? What would he care if her body crumbled like digestives onto the kitchen lino, a finger there, a big toe. An ear. A nipple found under the cat's dish. She can't remember now what she said to Declan. He probably hadn't even been listening. He'd wrapped up her container of ant poison as if it were an explosive.

'A curse, that's what they are', he'd said, 'Sure the whole estate is riddled with them. Riddled with the bastards. Pardon my French, of course', he'd added as an afterthought.

'Of course', she'd answered, barely able to look at him.

'Don't think you're on your own there Missus', he'd said, giving her a sly wink. 'The whole estate is on the move with them. Sure every woman in the place is scalded trying to keep them under control'.

He claimed to have sold at least half a dozen sprays the day before. Cora preferred the powder and told him so. She wanted to be able to see it on the ground, not have it invisible like a spray. Sprays were for cleaning windows or shining furniture. Sprays were for perfume squirted on the inside of wrists and the backs of ears before going out for an evening.

Handing her the brown wrapped package, Declan belched without apology, his stomach flipping over his trouser top like a deflated tyre. Cora paid him and took the package of death and destruction home.

'Mind your pets Missus', he'd shouted after her. Nothing about her child of course. Her Alice. Nothing about herself either. Or Frank, her husband. She supposed it would be okay if they got poisoned.

It has gotten to the stage where she can barely sleep. Her body bunches into a ball of tension. Minutes pass agonisingly slow. Death by poison would surely be quicker. Cora hates the nights. The fitful tossing, sounds of drunks going home, passing through the estates, going to their beds to sleep it off. Her bed is a pool of flat shadows where Frank should be but sometimes he doesn't come home.

'Drinking and driving don't mix', he says. 'You know that Sugar-bun'.

Again, she thinks if she had money she could go someplace. Take Alice with her. Let Frank be the one to squish ants under his thumb until they resemble blackberry jam or caviar. Let him be the one to pull out head lice, do the laundry, shop, take out the rubbish bin.

Those bastards were probably in the rubbish bin as well, eating their way through the remains of leftovers and dried out dinners. Fish, a little underdone, beef overcooked, tough as leather. But that's what you get from buying cheaper cuts. From trying to economise so they can save. Where was it getting her now? Poking and prising through special offer trolleys in the supermarket. Maybe she should start buying caviar, maybe then Frank would be at the table and Alice or herself wouldn't be trying to fill those awkward silences.

That afternoon, Cora trails what's left of the white powder around the circumference of the house. A white line of powder. Cora wonders if the ants are immune to the powder. Or if they'll get a high off it, sniffing it like cocaine. Some of the kids in the neighbourhood are on drugs she's been told. It's everywhere. Even the schools are full of drugs. She imagines kids in the corridors, their eyes rolling around in their heads, eyes black sunken dots. Cora has taken to looking in Alice's pockets. So far she's found nothing but fluff, sweet packets, chewing gum wrappers.

Frank is late again. Cora tosses and turns in the bed, her arms flailing out to his side of the bed. A thought comes to her. What if she goes downstairs now? Opens the kitchen door, a torch beam of light from the hall flooding in on top of them? Small squiggles of black ink moving over the white worktop. Dripping like words, sugary words off pages, sugar-bun words. Dripping together, whispering secrets. Like when she found that letter that time in his pocket before taking a jacket to be dry cleaned. A letter crushed into the corner of his inside pocket, balled up, creased. She could still make out what it said. The handwriting wasn't Frank's. It was small, spidery, crawling words over her skin.

Cora decides against going down. They'd become more cunning she was sure. They'd probably hear her step on the stairs, that creak on the third one from the bottom. They'd hide under a crack she hasn't noticed yet, a crack far too small for her body to squeeze down. They were probably down there now, at it like rabbits, multiplying. Cora shudders with disgust and closes her eyes. Her whole body tightens with rage. It doesn't last and when it goes she feels exhausted but still cannot sleep.

When Frank eventually comes home he undresses quietly, she'll give him that. No bumbling around the room or knocking over chairs. Before she can say anything, he's in the bed and asleep. He hasn't bothered to see if she's awake or not. Maybe she should dig her fingers into his ribs and ask him what he's playing at, coming home when he feels like it and stinking of perfume spray. But she doesn't. Instead, she imagines the white line of powder around the house. Maybe if she looks out her window she'll see other circles around other houses, luminous in the dark.

MACAW

Louise struggles to stay in the dreaming space but her daughter's persistent voice tugs her back from its weightless cocoon. She surfaces from underneath the duvet just as Lori herself appears around the bedroom door.

'Mam, it's Saturday and you promised ...' Lori looks even younger than her sixteen years. Her hair is swept in an up style, loose silky tendrils brushing her shoulders. Her fluffy dressing gown is pulled tight, revealing the curves of her slender body.

'Dad's been up ages and gone for bread, there's mould on what's left in the breadbin, yeuch!' A slight frown steals some of her prettiness.

'Sorry, I thought we had plenty', Louise says through a half yawn. Her head throbs a little. She's sorry now she'd had that third glass of wine and hates the lingering tang it leaves in her mouth.

'Dad will get lovely fresh rolls, he'll be back soon, and I'll shower and get dressed and be down in a minute, okay?'

'Okay. But don't forget your promise, it's Jo-Anne's sleepover next ...'

'Friday ... I know, as if I needed reminding, it's all you've been able to talk about ...'

'... and I don't want to look like a skaaanger ...' Lori interrupts, drawing out the word as if holding her breath, enjoying the look on her mother's face.

'What did I tell you about words like that?'

'You're just old fashioned Mam, everyone says it ... and you had your day on Wednesday, remember?'

'Just give me a few minutes, I need to shower first. I'll come down soon'. Lori nods then sticks her ear phones in, already mouthing the words of a song and bouncing her body out of the room. Louise flops her arm across to Dave's side of the bed, the sheet cold under her skin. A few hours earlier he'd reached for her, caressing the small of her back but when his hand moved along the length of her thigh she bucked her body against him. He'd turned away abruptly, falling into sleep again as she had, out-sleeping him by at least an hour she guessed from the quality of the light and the raucous sound of the neighbourhood 'barbers'. 'Saturday mowers, Lou, worse than Sunday drivers', Dave often says.

Hot water slicing over her back is a sensation Louise normally savours for as long as possible but her arms swish so fast with sponge and suds that her body is a blur, as if legs, belly and breasts belong to someone else. She sluices off the razor blade left on the soap tray. Lori began shaving her legs a few months before, despite the warnings it would grow back twice as thick and not necessarily blonde either. Un-wanted hair. Surely the bane of every woman's life? Like a secret, no knowing when it would find you out Louise thinks, rubbing steam from the mirror and plucking with her tweezers a stray hair from underneath her eyebrow line. Dave's voice drifts up to her. She imagines him filling the kettle, plugging it in, waltzing the cups to the table, adding side plates, cutting up the rolls, rubbing his hands briskly. She splashes a rush of cold water onto her face and rubs a towel over it vigorously until it stings.

'So ... what time are my girls off to town?' he asks, lifting the teapot and pouring the dark liquid into Louise's cup.

'I can give you a lift to the Luas, no problem'. Louise smiles at him, relieved he bears no outward grudge at least over her earlier rejection of him.

'I think we'll go local, I was in town the other day, I don't think I could face it again ...'

'And you came home empty handed, not even a pair of tights' Lori reminds her, shooting her mother a look of total bewilderment.

'I was meeting a friend', Louise says, busying herself with sugaring her tea. 'Not parading around shops'.

'Maybe you'll find something you like today', Dave says, stirring one full spoon into his own brew. His eyes meet hers across the breakfast table and for a fleeting moment his mouth tightens. But the moment passes and he recovers his good humour.

'Here Lou, have some more roll, you'll need all your strength'. He winks at Lori and playfully punches her shoulder. They eat in silence, each absorbed in their own thoughts, listening with half an ear to the news and weather forecast. There's a faint crackle but none of them move to adjust the tuning knob. Lori's expression clearly shows she's already in shopping paradise, her ear phones draped around her neck ready to be pushed into her ears the minute her breakfast's eaten. Despite her warm fleecy tracksuit Louise shivers. No matter what the position of the sun or the time of the year, there always seems to be a chill in the house, like cool to the touch cotton sheets. The sun just never reaches farther than half-way up the garden. Sometimes there's only the tiniest patch of it. Lori used to say, 'I'll pull down the sun for you Mam. I'll get a big lasso and pull it down towards the kitchen window until the whole place is toasting'. Was it only a year ago since Lori said that?'

'Been watching Bruce Almighty again have we?' Louise would say, tousling her daughter's hair. Lori was growing up for sure, moving into teenage bras, lipstick, 'growing her feathers', as her mother used say and testing out how much cheek she could get away with.

Louise looks at the pile of washing waiting in the laundry basket to be loaded into the machine and wonders if there's any powder left in the box. It's got a mermaid on the front, a sea woman with long hair and a big fishy tail, swishing about in a cloud of bubbles as if washdays were for blowing bubbles while the machine rocked from side to side, vibrating down through the floorboards. Nine out of ten women prefer this brand, so the jingle goes. Nine out of ten women prefer clear, perfectly formed bubbles that were just the right weight, the right buoyancy, resilient yet graceful.

'I'll run this lot through while you're gone', Dave says, noticing the direction of her gaze, 'No sweat'. He wipes his mouth with a paper napkin and slides out of the chair, turning off the radio with a grimace of disgust.

'Nothing only bad news as if there's not enough', he says, already gathering up the delph, stacking it neatly on the sink. He's all movement lately, hardly able to sit still long enough to eat. There's been talk of lay-offs in work, but as usual he's only told her the bare minimum.

Half an hour later Louise is sitting on a shoe shop bench watching Lori try on sneaker after sneaker. Lori tries on high heels too, 'just for the laugh', walking up and down as if auditioning for America's next top model. Lori could be on the red carpet she seems so poised, so unselfconscious. Like those gorgeous girls Louise saw on *The Golden Globes*. Beautiful, with low cut evening gowns. It still strikes her as funny in an odd sort of way. *The Golden Globes* on the television, in a waiting room filled with women just like herself, most of them around the same age, others young as Lori almost. Women with husbands or partners at their side, holding their hands or absently rubbing the inside of their wrists. Others like her, on their own. The silence, apart from the television droning, is stifling in the high ceilinged room. Louise is glad Dave's not there. She knows he's definitely not one of the nine out of ten husbands who prefer to be there ... even if he knew she was there in the first place. He wouldn't be happy sitting so still for so long. He'd fidget, need to go out for air or just to walk up and down the busy street watching taxis take off from or land at the kerb, as if they were aeroplanes at a busy terminal. He'd be shaking out cigarette after cigarette, blowing smoke all over passer-bys, the same way he did the night Lori was born. Louise was glad to be on her own in the grey carpeted, colour muted room, watching *The Golden Globes*, not knowing whether to laugh or cry.

'I really like these Mam ... Mam ... you haven't been listening to a word!' Lori nudges her arm, bringing Louise back into a shop full of shining shoes, unpaired, their partners in tissue packed boxes.

'We agreed on forty Euros max', she says, unable to keep tension out of her voice, 'These are nearly twice that'.

'They'll last twice as long Mam, you know they will', Lori replies in a wheedling tone.

'You get what you pay for', the assistant chips in, seizing the moment with years of professional practice behind her.

'You get what you pay for', Louise repeats as she punches in the number of her credit card with more force than she intended.

Two changing rooms later and each time she sees her daughter in another outfit Louise is reminded of an exotic bird, so painfully beautiful that to look at its startling shades hurts her eyes. The boutique fills up with other young women, glossy hair, pouting lips, their scent mingling in a heady cocktail. All of them wanting something new to wear, something that will show off their ripening curves, float them over their ordinary lives, at least for the weekend. Colours that brighten the dimmest nightclub and restaurant or swirling onto bedroom floors in the heat of a moment. Louise blushes, an old habit from years back that still plagues her. She lowers her head and hopes Lori hasn't noticed but already her daughter is gone behind the changing room curtain, shucking out of yet another outfit Louise decides is 'too old', for her. In the end, a compromise is reached.

'Thanks Mam, you're the best', Lori says when they reach home. Dave has the fire started which is a welcoming sight.

'Grateful enough to pull down the sun for me?' Louise asks. Her throat feels tight as if the old words are suddenly too big. Lori looks abashed but only for a moment. She playfully hugs her mother and says 'definitely!' before scampering upstairs with her treasures. Louise sinks into an armchair and eases her feet out of her shoes. She notices the shiny secateurs on the coffee table, its heavy silver head shaped like the beak of a parrot.

'It's time that overgrown triffid in the driveway got the chop Lou. It's practically out of control ... and scratching the side of the car', Dave says with a grimace. The car is his pride and joy, washed and polished religiously, rolled out like a limousine from their narrow driveway for taking Lori to sleepovers.

'Sit by the fire and warm yourself', he says, 'I'll be done before you know it. See if there's anything on the box for later'. She looks up at him and he seems to be a great distance above her, his head like a small, dark disc. Perhaps she could tell him now? But before she can say anything he takes up the secateurs, its size and shape making an awkward fit in his hand.

She closes her eyes, sees again the room with the chairs lined up against the wall, the acrid smell of geraniums drifting from the window sill, a smell reminding her of grief and anger. Her mother always had geraniums, her green fingers coaxing them from the smallest slips, dead heading faded blooms to encourage healthy plants. Their scent permeated the small council house she'd grown up in. Her mother died when Louise was in her teens, her body shrivelled, her illness detected too late to save her. Her father had shrivelled up too, and threw out all the geraniums saying he couldn't bear the sight of them.

She hears Lori moving around overhead, dancing her body into the small spaces between the furniture. Another sound comes, faint at first but as Dave moves nearer to the house, she hears the distinct clip of the steel cutting through the tender branches of her cotoneaster. She feels a sharp sensation in her right breast and her hand closes protectively around it. Its familiar softness surprises her briefly. What had she expected? Dave would be thorough, pruning back to the boundary wall, removing all unwanted leaf and bud, practicality over sentiment winning the day. She wonders what Clark Kent, at least that's what he looks like to her, is doing. Probably playing with his children, or just relaxing with his wife over a pre-dinner drink. Why shouldn't he? After all it was the weekend, he was only human, certainly no superman, no matter how much he resembled Clark Kent with his thick black hair and glasses. Why should he be sitting in his oak wood office on a Saturday afternoon, drawing diagrams for a virtual stranger? First a small circle then a biggish one as if an eclipse were taking place, one circle threatening to obliterate the other. He spoke in such measured tones they might be discussing the weather instead of the results of the call back screening, patterns of family history, statistics, choices of treatment, possible outcomes.

All the while he is speaking to her, Louise's eyes stray to the photos of his wife and children on the bookshelf behind his desk. Their faces lit up, the children wearing summer clothes, sailor type shirts and little pleated skirts. Perhaps the photo has been taken in their own backyard, sun flooding the whole way up, not just over a patch, barely big enough for a young girl like Lori to stand in, her head tilted back, temporarily out of reach from the shadows working their way relentlessly around her. Clarke's wife wears a straw hat that freckles her face. Louise will wear hats she decides, she couldn't bear the thought of someone else's hair. Or she will buy a bright turban the same shade as a scarlet macaw, its vivid colour startling the paleness of her skin. And they have good insurance, treatments were more advanced now. Her heart beats wildly at the thought of telling Dave. If not today, then definitely tomorrow she decides. When he eventually comes in from the garden, the secateurs are gripped in his hand, stray wisps of green trailing from the blade.

'That should hold it. For another while at least' he says, 'You know how Lori complains when it snags at her clothes'. Louise notices the tired look on his face, the awkward lean of his body against the doorframe. But she must tell him and now is as good a time as any. The ticking in her chest is like a time-bomb, so loud she thinks it will burst. Words form in her mouth, fragile, distorted, not the ones nine out of ten women prefer. Words that wobble and awkwardly teeter around the edges before breaking apart.

Put Your Shoes On, Susie, We're Going Out Tonight

Round and round it goes, like a whirlimejig in my head. Will it never let up? There's days it shuffles instead of whirling, and squeezes too. Like an old downpipe full of rust, the way my chest is after forty a day for forty years.

I first heard it whistled out in a bubbleful of spittle from McCann's mouth, then sung, right there in the butcher shop in Kiltimagh. McCann the 'Master' butcher with his big white coat and blood half moons under his fingernails and the big knife slicing into the hind quarters of a swinging cow. Singing and slicing and slicing and singing as if the shop were a ballroom with the gauze of girls white dresses and not a sawdust-strewn corpse emporium. McCann, big as Maghu himself, big as a bullock, shoulders the width of the Shannon and hands the size of hams. To hear him singing that song as he bent over the block! Christ that takes me back all right. And the thick neck on him, bulging out, a murder of a man, sure he'd have crushed any poor Susie if he'd had got a good hold of her.

I was a lad then, fourteen or so, long and lanky like a string of sausages, but with a full set of teeth and the blue of the western skies in my eyes. Blue as a river full of kingfishers. There was a fire in my belly too, and a young man's fiddle music in the long stride I took when I walked up the main street in Kiltimagh. I took McCann's song into my belly in 1949 and it lodged in my throat and in my head and down in the tips of my toes and all over my private places, and I brought it home to the house at the arse-end of that town where I lived with my father and mother, me being their cuckoo's flock, their one chick and a 'fucking disgrace' in the school, my father said, not being able to manage the simplest arithmetic.

McCann is long dead now, and eased out of the tune and into the next life. But look at the legacy he left me with? Those shoes belonging to Susie are still under my bed, behind the wardrobe, and they were in any suitcase I ever packed. Those shoes had walked the sands of Keel in Achill and left their prints there that were never washed away even though the seaweed strangled them. I was left with the words of a song about a woman who has as much substance as a ghost or a banshee crying over the long days and nights I spent in Cricklewood beyond. Cold as the china on a doll if ever there was a doll in that house, no sister in the house and my mother was not soft like that anyways if there had been a sister. She could twist the neck of a chicken quick as look at you – and often did, for the table, poor and all as it was when there was no work and violence might be served up as easy as a stew.

I've got that Susie around my back all right, like an albatross, she is. She's grown old and tired like I have, with her scraw of hair and her wizened face and woman's parts all dried up like the streets of Manhattan when I first went there. After I had gotten tired of vomiting up the night's drink in pubs all over Cricklewood, where there was nothing only the empty eyes of men I'd known, the concrete ingrained on their faces, hardening. There was plenty others went from here in Cricklewood and in New York too, neighbours and friends, leaving behind the prospects of nothing but walking the streets and hanging around corners with fags hanging out of their mouths and their hands stuck deep into their pockets.

McCann still sang though, drawing in his breath and letting it out like the steam of a train or the oar of a boat dipping the water … 'Put your shoes on Susie, we're going out tonight' … Christ, you'd think he was slip of a lad off to meet his sweetheart, with the promise of her breasts like two duck eggs warm from the nest trapped in his big hands, or the way he might press her slender bones into his big bull chest and crush her like a bird. But maybe when he sang that song it brought him out like a genie out of the tight neck of a bottle where he could float over Kiltimagh and hear the skittering of water hens in the rushes even. Without having to tear open the flesh of a spring lamp hardly weaned off the mother.

When I left Kiltimagh in the '50s I headed off for London. There were distant cousins there and we all mucked in together. The sweat we sweated would have flooded the Shannon, all those back-breaking hours bent over rocks and stones, the skin on our backs flailed with the heat. Anything I earned went on taking Susie out, buying her new shoes every Saturday down the market. I bought her slippers for dancing and strong brogues for walking the hills of Kiltimagh on the rare occasion I went home. I bought her sandals for the summer pavements that were white as the glare of the sun. And slippers for comfort, for putting her feet up of an evening and reading the paper or listening to the wireless or just for feeling the ease of the swelling in her ankles go down. We went back across the water, fit and tanned and sometimes I could even forget she was on the high stool beside me in the pub or left on the straight-backed chair in the corner of the bedsit. Sometimes, with bravado, I went down the markets on Saturday just to feel part of something, to hear the Cockneys banter with each other, to look shyly at girls with drindle dresses, their legs like swans.

Yet Susie was always there, a goddess then with golden hair and eyes the colour of the green hedging at the back of the school in Kiltimagh. And she kept her looks for a long time. Even when I was drunk, blind as Raftery himself wandering through the hills and vales, she kept her looks. Fresh and young as a chick, fluffed out in spring. She slept with me at night too, and drowned out the fist fights and the retching in the boarding house, and the smell of her cloaked the stench of piss and vomit and the scent of the wildflower that grew in the wetlands of Kiltimagh.

I heard the song over the soar of machines in a factory in Brooklyn. And me straightening the tie and slicking back the hair and sure even then no woman would look at me, never mind lie with me. Lashing in the porter, singing that song, Susie's tiny feet slipping into the glossiest slippers, glossy as the feathers on a bird. That kept me going. I held her small hand, small as the breast of a swallow, and she sat with me in the long hours that stretched across Manhattan skylines that looked like the wooden toy house I got every Christmas up to the age of eleven. Each block, each sharp angle having to fit the box. Each colour brighter than bright. Putting the pieces into the box, fitting each piece perfectly, while the fire was lit and the lamp burning. The radio on and the neighbours and their dogs quiet. No wind howling for men with Friday wage packets from the factories being thrown over bar counters. What was left was shaken out of pockets the next day or robbed while the men slept. Dipping the hand, the perfect size of the pocket, the white lining, the greyish white lining powdered with cigarette flakes.

When my father died – roaring, I heard after in the town – I came home, swinging in like a huge crane. It was January, the month my father was put in into the ground beside my mother, a woman who should have had a song herself to sing. I threw a few handfuls of clay on the wood and it fell soft as if Susie herself had thrown herself across the coffin and covered it with the silk of her hair. I never went back over the ocean, but Jesus, it's still hard to settle. Especially here where the song began. The song that still goes round in my head like a whirlimejig, round and round it goes like the dream of that woman, I once had, her eyes big drops of time.

For Soon-Ae-Kang

Old woman, you live out your days like so many others like you; memories from childhood withered in the gnarling of time. Other memories are livid as a fresh-made scar.

You live out what is left of your promise, in a house of shelter on a remote hillside in North Korea. A house that knows no violation only deep sighs murmuring into eventide's lengthening shadow.

Your hair no longer midnight shimmers, is no longer braided in the custom when footsteps were soft in your village, when hearts were full and all were free from threat. When the moon, full and round, dipped into the purse of night. A moon that glittered outside the hut where you were born, a lantern until sleep claimed you. But now, you can scarcely remember back to those solid days and nights. Where you were framed by the warmth of mother, father, brother.

You, in your seventy-fifth year, cannot take yourself out of your skin, cannot shuck off the rough touch of hands, the slither of tongues like serpents running over your flesh. What remains of your child-woman blossoming is a dried out husk, brown as oak. You can no longer think about the sight or scent of peach tree flowerings in a spring thaw. How a bud blossoms into its own small glory.

Soon-Ae-Kang, old woman from the Philippines, Land of Morning Calm, when I think of you like this, there is little that can soothe me. When I think of you, I see my own daughter's face, smooth yet fragile. My own little one who is the same age now that you were on that morning when soldiers took you from your father's house. Eleven summers old.

My daughter has the wind in her hair and the wind too is a young girl whose dance is as old as time. Light and frothy as air, her wisdom whispers along the whole length of a suburban garden, making light of the heaviness of concrete and towering houses. There are no corners she cannot skirt with ease, no sharp edges her touch cannot soften.

My daughter has the colours of the sea in her eyes. Colours that gleam the unexpected. In my daughter's fingers are carried the elements pinched in exact measurement to sprinkle joy. She is the promise in each new sunrise. From her lips fall rhyme songs that soothe my hurts. When she moves, a flock rises from the shore. Her hands fly out from her body with an energy that folds into the everyday of my ordinary. She is the bluebell vividness that surprises lonely places.

Soon-Ae-Kang, how well you knew those lonely places. Knew every hollow and bone celled in your bleak landscape. Those places have folded your hands into the shape of dead birds.

Today, I step out into the garden, into the day made fresh by the perfume of the wind. It wafts around my shoulders, wraps me in the silk of a caress that lifts the strands of my hair. I am opening into the embrace of branch and leaf, of crow feathers rising to display the fullness of their plumage. Caught and held here in a moment that reaches into my deepest self, I too am a child in the sway and thrall of morning. My heartbeat flutters its own tune in harmony with a low breeze skimming my bare knees.

Today my daughter goes for a burger with her friends. Food that you Soon-Ae-Kang probably never tasted. Her friends echo the sound of her laughter. My daughter will return with a red ketchup sauce ring around her mouth, the true telling of her innocent age, like the fresh line on the bark of a young tree. We will sit together in the gathering dusk of these last precious times before she crosses over to womanhood. She, eager to tell me all about her world and I, the eager listener. I am the rock that she leans against for shelter, I am the filigree of mist that spins her dreaming. Each new moon will torch our skies to light the way of our journey to that forked road that lies ahead, the parting. But that is a way off yet, like pathways on the other sides of mountains. Mountains we have yet to climb.

Soon-Ae-Kang, you never climbed those mountains. Never scaled the heights due to you alone. A Chinese Emperor and a war you had no making in decreed when your childhood ended, without bridge or stepping stone or bright lit lanterns strung out in celebration. Lanterns that would outshine the moon and stars, lit by your beauty. You were eleven years old when your childhood ended. Exchanged like so many others, some even younger, to become a military comfort woman. Comfort for the arms of soldiers who, by day, lived in the horror of war, who, by night, tried to forget; burying themselves in the sweet flesh of children. The oceans did not roar their disapproval. Trees did not wave angry fists. The birds of the air slid silent through their spaces. In faraway lands, dust did not stir up clouds of doubt but settled in the dry air. Such are the ways of war.

On that morning, your brother cowered in the corner of your hut, fearful of the rifle butt pressed into his side. Your brother, only one year older than you, his body bent like a broken tree. Your mother, father, numb with pain, freezing into each other, awaiting your return from the forest where you'd been sent in search of wood. The flame beneath your mother's cooking pot had long gone out and still no sign of you. Soldiers' voices filled the hut you'd known since babyhood, the home where you'd been carried near your mother's breast, where you took your first faltering steps, where you'd slept in the sling of the moon your father fashioned and wrapped around your sleeping.

Soon-Ae-Kang, you waited in the forest, glorying in the dance of dragonflies as they kicked up their heels to reel over juniper, bamboo, willow. A landscape alive and alert with reds and golds licking skywards. You were nudged gently by the wind as the forest blazed and your blood quickened you to sing the words of a child rhyme sung in your native tongue.

Soon-Ae-Kang, when I think of you like this, I see my daughter's face rise before me, how she glimmers with the possibility of all that she is, has yet to be. I see you reach the clearing in the long track that wound you into the forest like a silken scarf. It is mid-day and a hot sun beats down on your skin, your body tilting forward, a young sapling.

Now you see soldiers' trucks steaming in the village heat, hear their shouts of rage. You turn to run, not on the scarf path but deep into scraping branches that would rip the thin cloth of your dress, bruise your tender body. You would have run until your heart burst like the blossoms on the spring trees. I hear your breath, already rasping in your throat, struggling to find its rhythm. This you could have borne. You could have endured the deepest cuts, the weariest exhaustion. But then came the rustle of foliage, hands reaching out to grasp you to the ground, burying you into the hard, unforgiving earth. A soldier grates against you, the brass of his uniform a dull leaden sheen, like spit, on your skin. This is the last thing remembered before clouds of pain scud over the dark circle that blocks out the day.

Soon-Ae-Kang, you were eleven years old when your childhood ended, snatched from you by a soldier man boy from another country, a soldier whose own mouth was full of brutal emptiness. He was the first of many soldiers.

Half blind from tears, explosions of pain in the most secret part of you were pulled with others like cattle into a truck. Tarpaulin stretched tight across its metal bones. There were no farewells. Nothing but the mourning wail that rose up from the living and from the ghosts of your ancestors. Inside that metal truck, the outside world was shrouded in a black cloak. Fear palpated from the young girls you'd played with, who kept their eyes downcast as if not seeing would make this horror disappear.

On that journey from South Korea to the Philippines, you listened for Shaman whispers in the breezes. Whispers taught you in the ways of your people as I have taught my daughter, in the soft merge of an evening, to keep her angels safe on her shoulders. But there were no wings to lift you from your fate; the winds of war had spoken. A war of greed, with no place for wisdom or for angels. Over miles of road you travelled, along paths that could never be retraced. Rivers snaked below the hills where the sun hid. You were forbidden your father's honourable name, denied the very language of your birthright.

The stars that shone over that land lost their light. Clouds scraped over the face of the moon. To think of my own daughter, borne to an alien land by strangers, her sweet smile obliterated, the soft embrace she gives so readily, frozen by fear, the music of her voice shrunk into nothingness. To think of my daughter, my precious blood, with stained face, her eyes drained to pinholes. Nothing in her hands to hold but empty space. Not even the certainty of what lay ahead. What the morning would bring. But morning came for you, Soon-Ae-Kang, the first of many such mornings.

After a sleepless night spent in the tiny hut you were brought to, dawn filtered through slatted blinds. Your eyes searched for some small joy but there was nothing but mosquito net, rough blanket, washstand, bed. Nothing for the ear but heavy boots echoing across bare boards, the sound that followed upon that first knock upon the door which was the first of many. Nothing for the ear but the rusted creak of mattress. Then, you were unable to raise your spirits high enough above brass buttons on a uniform tearing into your flesh. You cried so much that in the end, each and every tooth was knocked from your mouth. Yet, still you cried. I see my daughter's gap toothed grin in photographs. The natural way of things has twisted itself into a coil that winds its weary loop about my throat, constricts it with unshed tears. My mouth is full of stones, carrying the weight of all these empty words.

Old woman, you live out your life in a house of shelter. Your hair no longer midnight shimmers. You cannot take yourself out of your skin. Cannot shuck off the rough touch of hands, the slither of tongues like serpents running over your flesh. You can no longer think about the sight or scent of peach tree flowerings in a spring thaw. Soon-Ae-Kang, when I think of you, I see my own daughter's face rise before me. My own daughter, who is the same age now as you were when you were taken from a place where dragonflies kicked up their heels, reeled over juniper and willow.

You were eleven years old when your childhood ended. Exchanged, like so many others, to become a military comfort woman. Essential supply.

THAT WOMAN

Evie remembers the last time. It was right there, on the back porch; that woman puffing her brains out at the time, watching a high wire act of swallows. Who'd want to be around some-one like her? A head the size of a football. Stuffed full. Eye-balling those birds getting ready for take off. That woman found a much easier way of getting up there. Sucking like a greedy hatchling out of Momma Bottle's throat. Squinting up into the afternoon sun as if looking through a monocle.

The last Evie saw of that woman was six weeks earlier, maybe a little more, a little less, it makes no difference. Her hair lanky, the taste of bitterness still fresh in her mouth, throat raw from one too many. Straight vodka to finish. To hell with those swallows with their peg-legs, not knowing which way to go, whether to stay or take off. She'd had her moments and without a safety net either. When the fall came though, it hurt. And why wouldn't it? Coming too in that terrible moment and then that horrible room. Roses and lilies rotting off the walls, bearing down on her like an army of corpses.

The look of disgust on Colm's face. Murder in his eyes. If he could, he would have pillowed that woman into oblivion while she slept. Who would blame him? And the kids picking their way around the house as if there were bombs under the wreckage, which there were. Breakfast would be okay. Colm never lost his appetite, no matter what that woman did. Or maybe it was just to be doing something. First the trip to the supermarket because that woman never had anything in. The fridge was always empty like her promises. Then, coming back with .the laden bags, fresh baked bread, tomatoes the colour of blood, the colour so bright it blurred her vision. The smell of the frying pan making her stomach heave. Yet, she forced herself into the chair through sheer will. She even managed to choke down a mouthful or two.

If only they'd go away. Two pairs of brown eyes watching her every move. Just babies really. Jesus how had it happened? Why couldn't she quit when she was ahead? The third or maybe the fourth drink? Those eyes. Staring at her. Pinholes. Adult fear in littlepeople bodies. Littlepeople that scattered like marbles when they saw which way the land lay. Hating her weaving after them. Her sour smell.

She remembers the dinky cars they'd played with. Streamlined, shiny, metallic. Not soft like the blue cardigans Evie knitted for her two baby boys. All those hours knitting identical cardigans with matching hats. Casting on, casting off. Then their dinky cars, zooming in and around the furniture. Whizzing under the table. Once or twice she'd fallen over one and screamed bloody murder. The frightened eyes that met hers could hardly penetrate her rage. A few times she'd fallen in the hall but she hadn't been able to blame the toys then. She'd laughed as she slid down, slurring against the side of the wall in slow motion.

That woman was a bad smell. The worst smell in the world.

Bottle. Long slender neck goosing out of the cupboards, her hand around its throat. Blood red wine spilling into a glass. Red on the tongue, teeth, the mouth. Red down the thin tunnel to where it sloshes around the inside of the stomach, a great wave roller-coasting the senses, rising in a wall of dizzying speed. Trying to keep a foothold then letting go, letting it all go … all the shadows melting back, kept at bay for a while, shadows that threatened to grab that woman by the throat and squeeze until there's nothing left.

Coming back from the edge is not a nice business. Especially when she was going out of business and was everybody else's business. The neighbour, always the neighbour who knows the shape in the bulge in the bag and what exactly the bag contains and even the clouds in the morning sky scurrying along with her as the weaving path is made from town to home, from railing to front door.

Once inside and the door is locked, the space opens out in a huge field with a cliff at the edge of it and a sheer drop. The risk of the drop is brilliant, thinking she could go near it but wouldn't fall. The field is dotted with bottle openers like daisies or pissabeds. There are bottle openers growing on the trees. Bottles in the presses on the walls, liquid filling her belly the way a tree fills out the sky or stretches up through the foot roots. Up through the cold knees, twisting into limbs and whorls and grains. The way a tree narrows in and widens out the waist and painful chest from all that smoking. In here, in the field behind the front door; from early morning she can uncork the lying down in the grass with the heat of the sun dancing off the peeled paint of the kitchen chairs and the naked light bulb yellowing under the fog of dust. Then the knocking on the door and she's just at the edge of the field where a big cliff leads down to a sheer drop of a million feet of nothingness but black midnight black and the sheer drop is all that's left in the bottle held by the neck. Choked and squeezed until the last drop trickles down the throat of an afternoon and then the knocking, the broken knocking, the wakening up but still asleep, the opening of the door but not being able to focus on the world outside. Everything swaying and skewed. The neighbour rocking from side to side. The neighbour's hair in rollers, slippers on her feet, the rest of the day in tatters with nothing in the cupboard but a pile of cobwebs.

Then staring into the face of this neighbour who normally wouldn't give that woman the time of day, now standing on her doorstep, doling out reproach, another belt in the face from the cold light of that awful coming too, squeezing and pushing everything away only back it comes and slaps her in the face. Then Colm comes home from work and finds that woman lying under the window like a dog or a cat, not a sound from her and a dribble of sourness at the side of her mouth.

That's how it happens. Even weeks later, when her hair's washed and her face is clean and she's able to walk without a stagger and open the milk carton without her hands shaking, it happens. Everything blows up in that woman's face. She's been to the room with the roses and stood up and said … no, confessed, her crimes. To a packed audience no less. She's done everything but wear a brand on her forehead and Jesus, she's had those regrets and the shame branding onto her flesh. Then, just as she starts to feel reasonably safe, he catches her eye one evening and all hell breaks loose. All the anger bottled up in him un-dams itself like a red flood pouring over her skin. It's not the shouts or the upturned tables or the clenched fists or the shaking shoulders that's so bad. It's the kids skulking off, like shadows sliding under the door, into corners, finding the smallest hiding places. And so it goes, into the night when sleep wants to come but is kept back with more shouts. Where's the neighbours then? Probably with a glass glued to the wall. The entertainment for the night screaming through the walls. To hell with them that woman shouts. Where were they when she was left on that back porch, her bare toes turning blue with the cold, bare concrete full of cigarette stubs. Everything overgrown around her. Weeds, nothing but choking weeds. Where were they then? Only hurrying by as fast as their legs could carry them for fear of contamination. Huddles of them on the street. Watching her make a slow progress up and down that miserable street. She supposed they thought it was only a matter of time before the white van would come for her and some-one would shove a doll in her arms and that's all she'd have left to rock, back and forth, back and forth, her eyes dead in her head.

But Evie got her back into the land of the living. She sat with that woman through all those meetings where grown men would cry and turn pale from the horrors of what they had done. Smashing up houses, breaking up furniture, breaking hearts. Robbing children of their childhood. Amazing how eloquent they were in those rooms. It was an outpouring of horror, sheer no-holds barred horror. But Evie took her there, lifted her up off that cold back porch step and sat with her until some sort of sanity returned. She supposed it was because of things that could be said there that couldn't be said anywhere else. After all, that woman couldn't ask the butcher for a half pound of sausages and then say: 'By the way, my head is hanging off me from the drink so I won't actually be eating your stupid sausages today', or, wanting to put herself into the mincer because that's how bad she felt. Outside the rooms with the roses rotting off the walls, the others, men and women, scattered like birdseed thrown to the winds. There was no standing around outside saying: 'Jesus, did you hear that … who'd believe that any human could do that to his wife and children?' Oh no, there was none of that. Maybe it'd be better if it was like that. If everyone had a good laugh. Jesus, imagine going into the bathroom sober and coming out elephants. Who wouldn't laugh at that? But no, it was all deadly serious. Getting well, getting better, getting on with her life but not unless she first told everyone what a monster she was. She couldn't lift that woman up from the back porch and take her there unless that was on the cards. Not like that either, barely able to stand up, thrown out of the house, puffing like crazy on a butt that made her sick to her stomach but still she kept sucking on it. She had to wait until there was some give in her bones, however hard it was. Then going home, it was hard to let go of all that, to go home and pretend your head wasn't full of horror. Horror soaked in alcohol, pickled with it. The smell of it was everywhere. Under the cushions, behind the cooker. Hanging from the roof like cobwebs.

The children crept around like shadows. Colm was like a ghost. Pale and grey in his coming and going. Leaving for work with his mouth twisted into the corners and coming back in a shroud of silence. Each time it took longer to string the words out of him, words that wound him back to some kind of normality. This time was no different. Six weeks of watching for the first signs of that string to be reeled out. Evie thinks that Colm knew this time there was nothing left only a place of no return, nothing only death or the turn for the way back. You see, Colm could still see that woman on the back porch step, still having to sidestep her as he went out to the clothesline while she poked around the weeds wondering if she could make a start.

THE MILLS OF GOD

When Moira and Brian return to their room the bed's freshly made up and the window's slightly open. Its yellowing shade of net curtain flutters like the frill of the waves. Theirs is a sea view, touted as one of the hotel's few selling points. A light breeze freshens a stale, lingering odour of cigarette smoke. Brian insisted on having a smoke earlier on despite Moira saying, 'There's plenty of lounge space in the hotel and you know how I hate the smell'. After all these years she still can't abide it and has absolutely forbidden him to smoke in certain areas of their terraced house on the outskirts of Dublin.

Brian sprawls on the bed, opening the drawer of the locker, lifting out the hotel folder and checking inside the plastic covers. The folder holds the usual leaflets telling where to find a doctor if there's an emergency or the location and price of a good curry, pedicure or wash and set. A menu for a Tandoori Sizzler Emporium further down the promenade slides from a slightly greasy centre fold, onto the brown and cream woven carpet that has 'seen better', as Moira put it when they arrived ten days earlier.

'All present and correct, right down to this five pounds', Brian says, counting the thin sheaf of money hidden in the folder and extracting the note, which he then folds carefully into his wallet and puts into the back pocket of the slacks he'll wear to dinner later on.

'We soon will be down to the last coin, we've spent a fortune, and nothing much to show for it only a wobblier belly and more than a few headaches', Moira says, tweaking the flesh around her waist through the fabric of her light summer dress. She moves to the window and removes the wooden block that holds it open. She'd noticed the broken sash the first evening they arrived and when she drew Brian's attention to it he'd gone downstairs, straight to the manager, insisting she go with him to her intense embarrassment.

'I'm not going to pay for damages already done', he'd said, highly indignant. The manager, a tall, thin, man on the cusp of middle age, assured Brian of 'The best possible attention at all times, day or night', and 'Of course sir, the window will be seen to immediately'. But it's still broken.

'What do you expect for cheap?' Moira says when Brian complains, 'what if it's docked from the deposit?' But even if he pretends not to hear her state the obvious, she can't help noticing the furniture in the room so heavy and dark or each time the toilet is flushed the sound is so loud it could be Niagara Falls gushing from the cistern with the long chain.

She closes the window, cushioning the blare of fairground music spinning around with chair-o-planes and swing boats. Closing the window seems more respectful also. It doesn't seem right to be listening to Bill Haley's 'Rock around the Clock', after what's happened. Moira can see, right there in the direct line of her vision, the fluorescent yellow and white markings of an ambulance on the strand where a crowd is gathering. The area immediately near the ambulance is cordoned off with red traffic cones. Just their luck it would have to be in front of their particular window. To her amazement, everything continues as normal outside of this area. Surfers are riding the waves and the Ferris Wheel, packed with sweethearts or settled married couples with kiddies in tow, continues to rotate, ever so slowly, as if it is turning the town on its head.

'Jesus, I'm not the better of it, are you?' she says now, removing her sandals and carrying them into the bathroom to rinse under the tap. She comes out again and lays out a fresh dress and clean underwear. She longs to bathe her feet and soak the towels which are wet and scratchy. The gritty feel of sand grates like slivers of glass against her skin and has lodged between her breasts and toes. It has even found its way into her belly button. All the deck chairs had been rented out when they'd eventually arrived on the strand some hours before, and so they'd been forced to lie on their towels, stretching them out as long as they could and turning and twisting on them like their pet Labrador Misty on the fireside rug.

'I could do with a large gin and tonic', she says now, her tone low and weary. She feels as if the very breath has gone out of her, now that they are away from events that have happened so fast.

'You need a stiff one alright', Brian says, looking at her as she shakes out her hair from the green rubber band. A spray of sand fine coats the bedspread and shakes like talcum powder onto the glass top of the dressing table. Moira is taken aback. There's no mistaking Brian's meaning or the look in his eye, and under normal circumstances she might be tempted but now? Surely not?

'I don't know how you can even think of going to bed after what's just happened'. It's a side of her husband she's never fully understood, his ability to detach himself from the most gruesome of situations. In Moira's book, lying on a Marks & Spencer stripy towel, trying to get a sun tan while a poor soul is stretched out, not two feet away, dead as a doornail, is undoubtedly one hell of a gruesome situation.

'Forget about him, his time was up and he croaked. End of'. Brian has a glazed look in his eye. He clearly hasn't yet given up on getting Moira into bed. The heat of the room and the smell of seaweed from her skin are making him more than a little eager.

'We've only got a few days left', he says, advancing towards her. We might as well make the most of it'. He comes close enough to touch her arm and bends to kiss her shoulder.

'I wouldn't be able to. Not now'. She shrugs him away. 'And there's no use going off into a sulk'.

'I suppose that means I'll just have to wait', Brian says belligerently, breaking away from her. He goes into the bathroom first even though he knows she can't bear sand in her hair and must be looking forward to a nice cool shower.

She sits on the wicker chair, waiting her turn. Keeping her back to the window, she tries to avoid looking at the dated wallpaper with its pattern of big alternating squares in shades of lime green and orange. Instead, she concentrates on the large painting of the Blue Stack Mountains, their familiar shape emerging from shrouds of mist. It has been Brian's idea to come to Bundoran for their twenty-seventh anniversary, despite her wanting to go to Spain like most of their friends. Even Wexford would have been preferable; at least it wasn't as far from Dublin as

Bundoran. She hated the queasy feeling she got from long car journeys.

'The last time we came to Bundoran we had a great time, didn't we? Remember?' was Brian's reply to her suggested holiday alternatives.

Moira didn't bother reminding him how long ago that had been and they'd had Ian and Rosa with them then, making sandcastles and eating sandwiches by the shore. The phone rings, jolting Moira from her thoughts. She holds it to her right ear, feeling the grit of sand on the plastic.

'Madam, so sorry to disturb you', the manager's voice is soft and condescending but with a distinctly official edge to it.

'The police would like a word with you and your husband. If you'd be good enough to come down they can interview you in my office'. Moira is stunned. How has a 'word' suddenly transformed to an 'interview'?

'We'll be down as soon as we've showered and changed', she says, putting the phone back on its cradle. She looks at herself in the mirror, at the worried frown creasing her forehead and the raw sunburn across the bridge of her nose. But of course she mustn't worry, it's only normal the police will wish to speak to them. The sound of the shower ceases abruptly so Moira knocks on the bathroom door to hurry him up. Brian comes out wearing nothing but a towel.

'Ah, changed your mind, I knew you wouldn't be able to resist me', he says. He reaches to pull her towards him, at the same time whipping away the towel around his waist. Moira is shocked to see he is fully aroused.

'It's the police, they want to see us, they're waiting downstairs this very minute'. Brian's erection deflates visibly before her eyes, like a party balloon the morning after the night before. He reaches for the towel, knotting it tightly in place again.

'Well that's a nice how do you do', he says, 'Wonder what the hell they want us for?' Moira thinks it's obvious what they want them for but holds her tongue.

Half an hour later, Police Officers Enright and Jones are introducing themselves, instantly becoming, for Moira at any rate, a confusion of identical uniforms and rosy young faces. They could be twins like her own Ian and Rosa, their hair clipped so tight it's a just a dark line below their peaked caps. Brian shakes hands with them, some of his confidence restored by their youth. Moira feels her face flushing and can barely look them in the eye. The image of her husband, naked and prancing around like a prize stallion upstairs comes to her mind unbidden. What would these young men think of them if they knew what their 'interview' had interrupted? She knows that, under ordinary circumstances, Brian, in that condition would not have taken no for an answer, even though she definitely wasn't in the mood. Maybe they're thinking that's what they were doing in any case; it has taken them so long to come down. Surely, it's not unreasonable to want to shower and change clothes after an afternoon lying on sand and under a burning sun?

'We can go into the Manager's office. It's private there. This will only take a few minutes; it's purely for the record', Officer Enright says. When they are seated, he takes out his notebook and asks their full names, addresses, occupation, and car registration.

'Standard, regulation information', he explains.

'Now, please go over the reporting of the dead man in as much detail as possible', he adds, looking directly at Brian.

'It was Moira here who first noticed, isn't that right dear?' Brian says, taking her hand in his and giving her his complete attention.

'Yes, I was the one who realised the poor man was dead', she confirms, nodding. Brian murmurs 'Poor soul', under his breath.

'How did you know?' Officer Jones asks, loosening his tie a little. Moira notices the faint ring of sweat under each of his armpits and guesses that his wife, or indeed his mother, has to steep his shirts.

'I just thought he was very still and not moving at all'. In fact, she had been resting on her elbows, her sunglasses perched on top of her head, trying to read without getting lotion all over the pages; when she first suspected something was wrong. It was the amount of flies on the man's legs that bothered her but she didn't want to say that in this small room with nothing but a couple of chairs, a desk and a filing cabinet … and four people squashed in. It would probably sound foolish and she feels mortified enough as it is.

'It just seemed like it to me. I realised … after a while … that he wasn't breathing', Moira continues. The man's face was hidden under a straw sunhat, yet, despite the number of flies crawling all over his legs, he never moved a muscle. Moira didn't think he could be so deeply asleep, especially with the music from the chip van so loud nearby and children squealing or crying on squares of coloured blankets all around them. Flies were for swatting, that much she knew. She had special lotion she sprayed on herself to keep insects from lighting on her skin. She was pale and freckled and a natural draw for them. She noticed how the flies crawled at will around the sun bleached hair on the man's legs and that one of his flip-flops had fallen off onto the sand while the other dangled precariously from his foot. Although she couldn't see his face she guessed he was an older man, his body bony and wrinkled around the thighs and elbows. Before she noticed the flies, she remembers thinking how lucky he was to have gotten a sun lounger which was a step up from the deckchair in terms of comfort and that if it weren't for Brian dawdling over lunch and having a third pint of lager, she might be on that very lounger instead of him. She now feels guilty for having the thought in the first place.

'That's all I can say really', she says, narrowing her shoulders and staring down at the wooden floor, which is so scratched that it looks whiplashed. Brian tightens his grip on her hand.

'And did you try and see if the man was alright?' she was being asked. 'What did you do then?'

Moira feels panic tightening behind her breastbone. The truth of the matter is she asked Brian to go and see if the man was breathing but he'd refused to budge.

'Of course he's alright, he's probably sleeping off a right banger of a hangover, leave the bugger alone', he'd said, burying his head back into his armpit. Brian didn't mind getting the full force of the sun on his body but he'd read somewhere that the sun was terribly aging and uses fake tan instead on his face. Moira buys it for him in the chemists and always has to explain, 'It's for a friend', when, without fail, the chemist shop assistant advises 'this shade is not right for your skin tone, madam, it's much too dark'.

'I told my husband, naturally, of course I did', she says, after a pause. Brian looks from his wife to the two officers who are both staring intently at him.

'Well … I assumed the man must be sleeping, I mean you don't expect to come to the seaside for a holiday and find a corpse in the deckchair beside you … do you?' he asks, taking out his handkerchief and dabbing awkwardly at his upper lip. Moira notices his face reddening under his fake tan. She feels an urge to laugh at the absurdity of it all. Again, the image of Brian rampant in the bedroom barely an hour after the discovery of the dead man comes to her. What if the officers knew that? Would they be shocked? Amused? And at their age too! She could see it almost as the headline in one of the tabloid newspapers and again, fights down the urge to laugh, chewing her lip and squeezing her thumbnail into the palm of her hand so as to prevent a nervous giggle from escaping.

'Did it not occur to you to check Sir?' Officer Enright continues. 'After all, the poor man might have been still alive and might not have been beyond help'. Moira recovers her composure and is about to protest but holds her tongue. There's no doubt whatsoever that the man was dead. And it wasn't just the flies that confirmed it. His body was completely still, his arms trailing down into the sand. The posture just didn't look right. She remembers now the half-eaten sandwich in a paper bag under the deckchair. It too was crawling with flies. Was that his last meal? It had churned up the large portion of greasy lasagne and chips she'd eaten for her lunch. How truly awful though, and terribly sad.

And there was something odd about the mouth. When the notion that something might be amiss came to her, Moira realised that there was an unhealthy tinge to the lips and that the man's face, what she could see of it, was a strange colour also, a mottling of sunburn and deathly pale. But now, she decides she will say nothing and leaves a gaping silence for Brian to fill. If they'd gone to Spain none of this would have happened. What was it her mother always used to say? Something about mills … yes, 'The mills of God … The mills of God grind slowly'.

Brian looks at her and there's a pleading expression in his eyes. Moira can read him like a book. This isn't the way it was supposed to be turning out. Brian would be wondering for sure what they are guilty of. More specifically, what he himself is guilty of? His earlier explanation in the bedroom of a man dying in the sun, 'A heart attack most like, too much booze and fags', didn't seem so simple now. She could see his expression becoming more and more belligerent, aggrieved that an innocent person like himself is suddenly being interrogated. He'd be wondering what she was playing at, why she wasn't defending him, backing him up.

'My wife raised the alarm at the nearest pub, I think you know that already', Brian says, recovering some of his composure.

'And when the ambulance came she gave them her details as requested, what more could we have done? The post mortem will confirm the time and cause of death'.

'But meantime, what did you do Sir? What did you do while your wife went for help? Did you think to check for a pulse? Or think of giving mouth to mouth?' Officer Jones cast an intense stare in Brian's direction which he takes to be accusatory.

'No, I did not … certainly not', Brian replies. 'It was perfectly plain that the gentleman in question was dead … and I have no training whatsoever in resuscitation … none, whatever. I waited for my wife to go for help and I stayed by the … remains … to make sure that nothing was touched or taken from his belongings. I noticed he had a gold watch and that his clothes were neatly folded nearby'.

The two officers exchange glances and write in their notebooks. Brian shifts about in his chair which fights against his weight and creaks in protest. Moira can see he's annoyed at the suggestion that he should have checked for signs of life, or heaven forbid, given mouth to mouth. Worst of all, angry with himself for mentioning the watch and the crumpled pile of clothes beside the deceased man.

'That's it for now, you've been most helpful. We know where to find you if there's any further enquiries', Officer Jones says, sliding his pen in the plastic brackets holding his notebook together.

'Enjoy the rest of your holidays. We'll be in touch if there's anything further'.

'Be in touch. What on earth for?' Brian says when, five minutes later, they are outside the hotel and well out of earshot of the manager who gives them a very strange look as they step into the revolving front door in the foyer. The light is now fading from the day and coloured bulbs strung on wires along the promenade breathe like a pulse, glimmering shades of violets, blues and glaring reds. Elvis singing 'Heartbreak Hotel', drifts out from the slot machine arcade nearby before stretching beyond the swarm of children and adults still queuing up for king size cornets topped with thick chocolate flakes. The police officers have headed off in a different direction towards the station.

'They're probably going over everything we've said with a fine tooth comb', Brian adds. There's an ugly crimson creeping up his neck like a poisonous vine.

'And that watch. What if one of the quick thinking medics whipped it off, thank-you-very-much-that-will-do-me nicely sir. Or the mortuary assistant. What if he whipped it off? Christ, I can just see the white ring around that bugger's wrist'.

'Like a glow worm in the dark', Moira can't resist saying. 'Come on, we could both do with a drink'. Her tone softens and she links her arm through his. She honestly doesn't think they'll hear any further.

'Look, the surfers are still out', she says, pointing towards a group of wet-suited teenagers cresting the waves.

'And the Ferris Wheel is still turning; maybe we'll catch a ride on it later'.

'You've certainly changed your tune', he says, turning to face her, 'One minute you're the mother of sorrows because a stranger has snuffed it and now you're looking for Ferris Wheel rides. If that bugger's watch is missing, it's me they'll come looking for. Do you not realise that? Jesus, I wish now we had gone to Wexford'. And after a pause during which he kicks a loose pebble and looks at her sidelong, he adds, 'Or Spain'.

'Maybe we'll go there next year', Moira says. 'There are some great packages, and... Ian and Rosa might come too. We could rent an apartment big enough for all of us', she adds coyly.

'Anywhere but here, that's for sure', he replies, taking out his cigarette case and shaking one out.

'It'll be fine. It'll all work out fine, you'll see', Moira says, patting his arm.

'Whoever that poor soul is will have been long identified and his people sent for. We won't hear another word about it'.

She looks across the strand at the moon brightening towards the night and the Ferris Wheel circling the sky as if a giant, unseen hand is lifting its occupants high over the town where, however briefly, they can gaze out across the vast expanse of the sea and skim the rooftops before being lowered gently once more.

GUIDE

'Sharon might be delayed', the young woman is saying, 'There's always a traffic buzz at this hour'.

'It's not too late to cancel, I don't mind', he says. 'No need to trouble her for just one person'.

'Sharon's taken tours for one before, no sweat'. Mike notices a tiny piece of chewing gum bob under her soft pink tongue.

'I can come back another day'. The lie comes easily to him. This time tomorrow himself and Edie would be well on the road to Cobh. But the young woman is insistent.

'No worries. Besides, visitors are scarce at end of summer'.

'In that case, who am I to argue?' he says, throwing his hands in the air in a gesture of mock defeat. He now has a name for the tour guide, matching it up with Stone, the actress he's had a crush on since he saw her in *Total Recall*. Still, he doubts if Sharon the guide will be anything like Sharon the actress.

He tries not to stare in the direction of the young woman at the cash desk; all peachy and creamy in a sleeveless short dress. Chewing her small wad of gum, oblivious to him; blowing small transparent bubbles, snapping them back into her mouth before they collapse over her face. And if she gives a thought for the middle-aged man shuffling through flyers, Mike reckons it's probably along the lines of how pathetic he is, on a tour for one. It must be a bit like eating a T.V. dinner for the guide. Maybe he should have gone on the boat trip after all even if his sea legs have always been on the shaky side.

'You can't be as sick as you make out', Edie said to him earlier at the harbour wall. Look, those little kids are going'. She'd stabbed her finger towards a family band trouping on board the small cruiser, the father carrying a toddler on his shoulders, the mother holding hands with a little boy. 'I'll barely be a mile from shore when I'll be spewing like a fountain'.

'I'll text as soon as I'm on the way back'. There was little warmth in her tone and the last he saw was the back of her red floral raincoat and her brown hair whipping about in the breeze.

Perhaps Sharon will be a bantam hen type? Mike once enjoyed those flashes of anger, Edie's normally pale face filling up with colour and her eyes sparking. Funny that. What once was attractive to him now brings on panic attacks. His blood pressure's up too and his cholesterol's high. If he cuts out anything else in his diet, he'll be eating cardboard. He picks up a piece of pottery stamped with the name of a neighbouring town, turns it over and then puts it down again. The usual Leprechaun Chic. What really surprises him though is the size of the tourist office. The blue and white building looks much bigger from the outside.

Mike's thoughts stray back to Sharon. This time, a steely-eyed, grey haired witch emerges in his imagination. Retired schoolteacher most likely, unable to resist the lure of lecturing to a captive audience.

A toothache, begun earlier that morning, nags at him afresh and he feels in his pocket for the bottle of clove oil recommended by the chemist. There's such a strong smell from it he hasn't used it yet. Just as he's about to uncap the bottle, the young assistant peers out the window through a chink in a display of lucky horseshoes and plastic colleens and calls over to him, 'Here she is, hardly late at all'. She gives Mike the thumbs up sign. Mike puts the bottle back into his pocket.

The light darkens into a pool of shadow at the doorway so when Sharon makes her entrance, he can't quite make out the face, just a silhouette which is surprisingly tall and slim. She shakes out her umbrella and leaves it to drip in the stand at the doorway before coming under the full glare of the fluorescent lighting. Mike feels the breath go out of him. Sharon, even if her hair colour is a few shades lighter, is the living image of his dead wife Martha.

'Hi', Sharon calls out a general greeting then makes her way to the counter, chatting briefly with the young woman at the cash desk. They lower their voices and Mike supposes it's to confer about him, a tall man with greying hair, wearing brown slacks and navy shoes. Sharon's voice gives him a shock also. Low and throaty, she even sounds like Martha.

He moves towards the door, planning a quick exit. It seemed to be the day for optical illusions but this was becoming too strange for words. Sharon stops him in his tracks with a wave of her hand, a movement that shakes the rows of bracelets on her arms, jangling them against each other. She lowers her arm and they slide back into place again.

'I'm Sharon, your guide for today'. Up close, Mike sees that her eyes are brown and not blue and her nose is slightly broader. Still, the resemblance to Martha is uncanny enough to send a shiver down his spine. Sharon steers him towards the back of the room and steps through a side opening he hadn't noticed. Her strappy sandals show bare brown toes and her spiky heels clatter on the stone floor as they enter the alcove. The space is filled with large boards hung from the ceiling like the sails of a ship, a reminder that Edie is heading further out to sea with each passing moment.

'This explains how the building looks so much bigger from the outside'. He decides not to mention anything about her being the spit and image of his dead wife.

'It gets missed. Lots. There really ought to be a bigger sign. The tour should take about an hour, okay?'

'Weather permitting', Mike says, not quiet meeting her gaze.

She points towards a name on the first large board, reeling off facts about the Norman invasion. Facts he hears with half an ear, becoming absorbed by Sharon's gestures and body language; they remind him so much of Martha tossing back her hair or hunching up her shoulders ever so slightly to minimise her height. On top of everything else, his toothache is still nagging. He's annoyed for not putting the oil on earlier and now it's too late. If Sharon really was Martha, she wouldn't care a damn about the strong smell of cloves. But perhaps Martha should have put her foot down a bit more; maybe she had been too easy going. The criticism gives him a pang of guilt. The truth of the matter was if he hadn't been so late home the day Martha died, he might have been in time to call an ambulance.

'See this guy? Sharon asks, interrupting his thoughts. She points to a large portrait of a man decorated in ruffles. 'A rake for sure, a real ladies' man. Coming in, throwing his money around as if there was no tomorrow, buying up land and parcelling it out to his relatives'. Her eyes flash. 'Relatives who were nothing better than greedy parasites'.

Mike nods. He could relate to that. Edie's family were always on the scrounge. Especially her brother, unemployed yet living the life of a country squire. He shifts his weight from one foot to the other which does nothing for his back. He hadn't reckoned on such a lengthy historical prelude and Sharon reminding him of Martha was definitely not part of his tour plan. After five years, he'd thought the business of 'moving on', as Edie put it, was behind him.

They're standing before the fourth board when the smell hits him. At first, he can't quite put his finger on what it might be. Sharon purses her mouth even tighter and stares at a very large image of Elizabeth 11.

'All that squabbling over this homely looking old broad. And bald with it. If she was an ordinary woman on the street, Walter wouldn't have given her the time of day'. She sighs, collapsing her shoulders. 'And in the end, he lost his head all the same'.

'Love does strange things to us all', Mike says, staring down at the floor.

'Lots of people who live in this town still don't even know who Raleigh was', she says, ignoring his remark. Can you believe it?'

'Maybe they think he invented the bicycle', Mike says and she smiles. But that smell! He assumes it must be her perfume. It's hard to know with scent, there's such an amount of alcohol in it anyway. The more he focuses, however, the more he's convinced of its real origin. Booze. Each time Sharon turns to him and opens her mouth, he's doused in it. Surprise turns to shock. It's barely eleven o'clock in the morning.

Now that he looks at her more closely, the strawberry colour on her mouth seems to have stumbled a little over the lip-line, like the crooked seams of a pair of stocking. Edie's mouth is small but beautifully shaped. A kissing mouth he'd told her when they first met and she hadn't minded his moustache. Lately, she's complaining of it being prickly. He touches it and feels reassured by its presence. Martha had thought it made him look dashing.

'C'mon, let me show you something', Sharon says, swinging around and heading towards the only window set into the back wall, up three steps on an iron stairs. Narrow and wide, the view from the window looks out over the harbour where several boats are tied up.

'Sand bars. That's what killed this harbour. Putting an end to the great voyages. And two important power commodities'.

'Which were?' Mike feels obliged to ask. The smell wafts to him, even stronger now.

'Salt and spice. That's what it took back then to wield the stick. Salt to preserve and spice, well, spice is spice'. She leans down, pressing her hands into the sill, her body seeming to sag a little. Looking at her makes him think of Martha taking her last breath, probably murmuring his name as she did so. And on the same day he'd made up his mind to tell her about Edie. How ironic was that? A 'silver lining' Edie said at the time, 'At least Martha died thinking you loved her'.

'Have you seen the lighthouse further up?' Sharon asks him.

'Yes, it's an impressive sight along the promenade, especially at night'. The rhythmic throb of the lighthouse reminds him of a big red beating heart. His own 'ticker' scare has certainly put an end to some of the spice in his relationship with Edie. He's beginning to wonder how long it will be before Edie calls it a day. The thought doesn't exactly devastate him as much as cause him to think about his own future. His text messaging goes off. Sharon waits for him at the entrance to the alcove while he fishes out his mobile. The text is short and to the point. The boat trip would be longer than expected. Edie had timed the boat trip and the walking tour to coincide more or less and now she'd be crabby when she returned.

'Let's go', Sharon says, clattering out of the alcove towards the front entrance, retrieving her umbrella on the way out. Rainfall is light but he yanks up his hood and tightens it around his face by pulling at the cords on either side.

Now they are out in the air, the smell seems to fade and as Sharon strides ahead of him across the road Mike again wonders if he's imagined it.

They walk along the street pausing at focal points of interest. Towers and almshouses. There seemed to Mike to be more of the old than the new in the town. Sharon nods in recognition at several people they meet along the footpaths.

'You must know everyone here', he says.

'It comes with the territory. This place is like a goldfish bowl'.

'Small town living, it's the same everywhere', he replies.

Out of the artificial light of the tourist office, Sharon looks older than he first thought, but her eyes are focused and her words perfectly formed. There's no slurring, definitely. Once more, he's struck by her physical resemblance to his dead wife. It's there in the wide forehead and the mouth most of all. The desire to tell her is overwhelming but he realises it might sound like a chat up line. And at his age too. Bad enough he has a partner so much younger than himself. No fool like an old fool he can almost hear Martha saying. Just as well she never did find out about Edie. Again, he feels a stab of guilt. The shock of finding Martha sprawled on the floor like that. Tumbling off a chair while changing a light bulb seemed such a freakish way to exit the world. Not at all dignified, or fitting for a woman like her.

'These walls date back to the 12th century and some of the houses around here are exactly as they were then'. Sharon points to what's left of the original boundary walls and although she must have seen them countless times she manages to inject a sense of enthusiasm into her voice.

There it was again. He can still hardly believe that a woman about to meet the public would pour herself a drink so soon after getting out of bed. If it weren't for him and the tour, she'd probably be loaded now.

They pass by a bakery shop. In the window there's a pyramid of luscious cakes smothered in cream. The cakes are already thickly sliced, ready to eat, even more tempting. Mike's mouth begins to water. It seems ages since breakfast which was really only a cup of tea and a half slice of toast. If his heart condition ruled out luscious egg and bacon, the threat of full blown toothache definitely did not stretch to sugar laced confectionary. And the clove oil wasn't the cure, the chemist made that perfectly clear. He sees a fly about to land in the middle of a nest of coconut. Eating a slice of anything in that window would be like playing Russian roulette with a king size stomach bug. Death by coconut. If Martha were here, she'd be linking her arm through his and laughing along with him.

'Death by coconut', he says to Sharon, pointing towards the window. She looks at him blankly and shrugs. Not even the ghost of a smile.

A man in shirtsleeves, lounging in a pub doorway across the road, blows a kiss over to Sharon. 'Old rogue, he never quits. Still thinks he's Casanova', she says with scorn in her voice but she blows a kiss right back.

She strides ahead of him on the narrow footpath, past the Post Office and the Bank.

'I'm going to call it quits here', Sharon says, coming to a halt at a very old wooden door curved in an arch. She tells him it's the original entrance to a Benedictine monastery.

'Neat, isn't it?' She points to the long, narrow corridor inside where seats are positioned to make the very most of the space.

'And now it's a bar. Wonder what the monks would make of that?' Mike replies, peering into the near darkness beyond.

'Nothing stays the same, no matter how hard we fight it'. She runs her hands through her hair in a distracted way. 'Who knows, the monks might very well approve. It's been a pleasure but this is where I say goodbye'.

Mike thinks about tipping but it would be embarrassing counting out notes and besides, he only has some loose coins in his pocket. And a bottle of clove oil. He finds its presence is reassuring, even if it's only a temporary solution. Maybe he could buy Sharon a cup of coffee … or something … but before he can ask, she's already half way down the long corridor, stepping into the past.

OUR LADY OF CLONFERT

'They're finally having a mark-down', Bridget observes, breaking a silence that's lasted all of the two kilometre stretch from her front gate to Carleton's Fashion Emporium. 'Isn't that where you bought your pink two-piece Margie?' She turns her head towards her sister in the driving seat. Margie barely nods and tightens her grip on the steering wheel.

'You must have good sales in that fancy store of yours in Willesden'. Margie glances in the rear view mirror at Sally, the youngest of the sisters. 'Or are they too grand over there?' Sally gives her a smile in return but the blue of Margie's eyes is cold as chrome.

'Everyone wants a bargain. When the sale is on we can barely keep stock on the rails'. Sally has a distinct twang, as Bridget calls it, yet there are still traces of the Midlands in her voice.

'Some of the stock in Carleton's is as old as Methuselah. "Emporium" my arse', Bridget says. 'Lucky I was able to get cheaper and nicer in Fahy's for our Sean's wedding.

But if you've held onto your own receipt Margie, I'm sure they'll exchange it for something else'. She fidgets about in her pocket, finds a tissue and dabs at her nose. 'Or maybe you could still wear it to Sean's wedding; it's not that mother of the bride looking, if I remember rightly'.

Margie accelerates up the main street, past the supermarket and on towards the hotel near the end of the town.

'I heard this place is closed down', Sally remarks as a large sepia bricked building comes into sight. Her nephew Sean is a subject she doesn't care to dwell on, especially after what was told to her the other night.

'It already has the mean look of empty rooms, I suppose it was bound to happen', Margie says. 'With half the town emigrated and the other half in its dotage'.

'Even Sean's wedding, big and all as it will be, couldn't save that heap of rubble. We'll still have a great outing in Galway'. Bridget appears to be unaware of the resentment swelling like a blister into the physical space between herself and Margie who squirts up a jet of water over a splat of bird droppings on the windscreen and slashes the wipers over it.

Sally winds down her window. 'Think I'll let some Shannon air in, it's good to feel the fine weather on our bones'.

The two women in the front nod their approval. Both are wearing scarves, Margie out of habit and convenience, Bridget because hers is silk, given to her as a recent present for her sixtieth birthday. Sally can already imagine Bridget removing her scarf when they reach Clonfert, only to smooth it back on again, another irritation for Margie who often wears her scarf so she won't have to wash her hair so much, not caring if her greying mop springs out like a furze bush or lies flat across her head.

Over the bridge at the west end of the Shannon the smell of the river drifts in. Boats on the water dip and bob, barely disturbing its placid surface. An elderly couple recline on the deck of a small barge drinking from mugs and looking out into the far distance where the hay meadows are spread out. Their glossy coated black hound bends to drink from a bowl of water and as he does, his ears fold back to reveal pale pink linings. Sally thinks of silky evening gloves, a best seller at Christmas and the party season when she'd be rushed off her feet in the large department store in Willesden. 'Peaceful here, isn't it?' she says, gazing at the untroubled surface of the river. Both Margie and Bridget make a hurried sign of the cross.

'A man was three days missing before they fished him out of that same water', Margie says, 'He was never right in the head, the poor unfortunate creature. Money troubles they say but sure we all have to cut our cloth'.

'The Council closed the diving area years ago at least', Bridget says. 'No harm at all. When I think how Sean used jump off the bridge into the river, it still upends the heart in me. Thank God he never came to harm and turned out to be such a great catch. There's not too many the beat of him around here'.

'The corncrakes must be all but extinct', Sally says. 'One time you'd hear them as loud as bullfrogs'.

'There's still a lot of life in those grasses, don't be fooled, thick with the larks and the cow parsley, yellow as clots of butter in the summer time. Husbands are a bit extinct too, by the looks of it', Bridget can't resist adding. She sneaks a sidelong glance at Margie who presses her foot even harder on the pedal.

'Bridget, that's a bit uncalled for', Sally says, when her chest feels less tight, 'You know poor Grainne's heart is broken'.

'And for all we know, it could just be a lover's tiff; they might be as great as ever they were next week'. But Margie's tone lacks any real belief.

'By the time we've finished our devotions I'm sure everything will just fall into place'. Bridget leans forward and pulls down the mirror over the glove box and checks that her front teeth are free of lipstick. Sally wonders if Bridget and Margie realise how lucky they are to have children at all and to have lived close to each other all their lives, sharing joys as well as sorrows. With neither chick nor child Bridget often wonders what she has to show for all the years spent in London. If she hadn't loved her job so much in the bright store near her flat she might have come home years ago instead of only now considering the move as a retirement plan. It crosses her mind, not for the first time either, that maybe this constant sniping between Margie and Bridget has developed precisely because they are always in each other's pockets. But she'll be keeping that observation to herself. Least said was indeed soonest mended as they were fond of saying around these parts.

'You've gone very quiet Sally', Margie says, five miles later. 'Maybe you're getting ready for devotions, is that it?' There's a jeering note in Margie's voice. Bridget has rattled her and she also suspects that Sally is no longer a regular church goer, if in fact she goes at all.

'I know lots of people swear by the May visitations', Bridget says. 'It brings luck for the whole year'.

Not so lucky for that poor girl, Sally is tempted to say, left in a stupor, sitting on an empty crate near a laneway, full of alcohol and a stranger's juices seeping out of her.

'Well, we can all do with a bit of luck'. Margie relaxes her shoulders. For now at least she is prepared to leave aside Bridget's gloating that it's her Sean and not her own daughter Grainne who'll make it up the aisle first.

'Remember, we have to go three times to the devotions for our wish to come true', Margie adds. 'Or, if we like, we can just go in and come out of the church three times in the one evening'.

'That suits me', Bridget agrees, 'Otherwise, we'll miss Coronation Street'.

Along the banks of the river, fishermen stand with their lines cast, their bodies still.

'The Mayfly's rising, wouldn't you know, it must take great patience to stand for that length of time'. Sally is half tempted to wave at the men but doesn't.

'Look at all the hours you've stood in that store beyond', Margie says, 'Bless your energies, I couldn't do it, no matter how glamorous the stock or how posh the customers'.

'Many's the one was left running out of patience at the altar don't forget. At least Grainne can count her blessings it didn't get that far'. Bridget raises her hand, giving a Royal Queen Mum type wave to the fishermen absorbed in their task. Margie barely slows down as they arrive into Esker, watching for the turn at the old, disused school house. Another couple of miles take them to the crossroads and then the right turn for Clonfert. A magpie on the road pecking at cattle dung barely makes it airborne as Margie gears up again and the car roars on.

'Easy Margie, or we'll be going to Clonfert in a box'. Bridget clutches the side of her seat. 'I was just going to salute that fellah, that's what you're supposed to do when you see a single magpie'.

After a pause Margie says, 'maybe he's not single at all, for all we know he might have a wife … and a mistress too!' All three sisters laugh, awkwardly at first then full-bellied. Margie's quick wittedness makes it seem like old times when they were young, trying to best each other with jokes.

'Nice one Margie', Bridget concedes, wiping tears of mirth from her eyes and, before she can take the ball and run it elsewhere, Sally points towards a blaze of white flowers along the hedges.

'Would you look at the May bush, has it ever been so white? It's a sure sign of the First Holy Communion season. Were we ever that innocent?'

'If we were even then'. Margie takes her hand off the wheel and points towards the glove box. 'There are lozenges in there Bridget, I don't know about the rest of you but my throat is dry as last week's mutton'. Soon all three are sucking on the lozenges, the scent of oranges and lemons drifting around them as they reach the turn that takes them to their destination. Margie swings the car towards the entrance of a temporary car park, a field where a steward dressed in a luminous yellow vest is directing the traffic.

'We all have orange stripes no doubt', Sally says, flicking out her tongue.

'There'll be no Communion anyways. Whatever about what's on your tongue, make sure there's no cow dung on your shoes or the car will stink going home', Margie warns as all three step out onto the spongy grass.

'Did you see that Dermot Ryan as we came in?' Bridget asks, 'You'd think he was a film star the way he's cracking jokes at everyone and swinging his arms like a gorilla. I don't know how he can show his face after what his pup of a young fellah did to that poor girl'.

'You've only got Sean's word for that and you know how men talk in the pubs', Margie says. Everything's embroidered like the alter cloths in the church. Besides, this is no place for thoughts like that.

It's on the tip of Sally's tongue to ask why Sean hadn't gone straight to the guards, even now it wouldn't be too late, but she says nothing. Least said soonest mended.

What was it only talk and drunken talk at that? Still, better Bridget had not told her. It turns her stomach thinking about that poor girl, out of her mind with drink and 'interfered with' as Bridget put it, by Dermot Ryan's son when he was supposed to be looking out for her.

'I should have left you both out on the gravel path at the gate there', Margie says. 'The fields around here are marshy, winter and summer. I don't think it ever sees a rib of sunshine'.

'Don't forget we were born and reared in the bog', Bridget says, 'And we'll probably die in it as well'. Margie and Bridget laugh but Sally barely manages a weak smile. The sisters pick their way through the thin spaces between cars. Some are parked haphazardly, others in neat rows. They are also careful to avoid large pats of cow-dung. Bridget removes her scarf and smoothes down her hair before readjusting the silk, tying it neatly under her chin. 'Hold on a sec', she says, taking out her powder compact and checking her lipstick is still fresh.

Margie rolls her eyes but a fair amount of warmth has returned to them. 'Maybe Grainne has had a lucky escape', Sally says as they wait for their sister. 'Much worse things might happen her'. Margie nods and squeezes Sally's elbow. Bridget joins them and they pick their way through the grass. When they reach the gates of the field just across from the church, they can hear the familiar strains of the hymn *Queen of the May* drift out from the open door. Dermot Ryan, a man they all danced with as teenagers, is weaving about and signalling in even more cars with his big hands. 'He's still light on his feet anyway', Margie says, 'Even if there's not much going on in the brains department'.

'Unlike that son of his', Bridget says, 'Seems like he prefers to use a different part of his anatomy with women'. Again, Sally is tempted to raise the subject of Sean's lack of moral fibre when Ryan's son had boasted to him of his deed. Sally could well imagine Sean recounting the grisly tale to his mother, the two of them drinking cups of scalding hot tea by the range; Sean telling the news from the town like an old hen that has gathered up any crumb of gossip.

Dermot looks at the sisters as they approach and his expression softens. 'Ah, it's the Maguire girls! As good looking as I remember'. Sally knows full well she isn't the 'girl' of over thirty years before, but as the others draw near, his eyes remain on her face. She supposes there must be some remnants left from that time when they all threw shapes together and thought they were great. 'Are you still beyond in London?' he asks, not missing a beat with his hand signals. But he doesn't wait for her answer, redirecting a car headed towards a field that's already full. He dances before the car with his arms outstretched as if herding a cow broken loose from the bunch. For a moment she imagines him in the Hammersmith Palais where she herself danced for years. He'd have fitted in there alright with all the other Irish men that thronged around the walls on Saturday nights, drenched in sweat and burning up under the heat of the lights and the crowds. She wonders if Dermot knows about his son. Perhaps the deed was boasted of to him also? Surely not though. How could he be such a hypocrite, directing traffic for the May devotions? She follows after her sisters.

When she reaches the door of the church a blaze of candlelight blurs her vision and it takes a minute or two to find her bearings. Room is made for her in a nearby pew and she accepts the space. It's the women's night of the devotions. Mothers and grandmothers move their lips, fingering rosaries. Most of the younger women are accompanied by little girls sitting in their buggies. Some have dolls with missing arms, playing a game inspired by the statue in the centre of the church, covered by a glass dome; a statue made of wood that had lain hidden for centuries, losing an arm when a woodcutter hacked through the trees. Blood was supposed to have flowed with the severing. There are babies too, rosy cheeked and drowsy.

Sally glances around her at the faces of these women, their lips moving rhythmically in prayer, fingers weaving through rosary beads. Women who were part and parcel of their tribe; who've left apple tarts cooling on window sills or clean shirts airing in the cupboards. She gazes at the children, daughters who might possibly be at the mercy of a man like Ryan's son someday, when they least expected it. And Sean. Was he any better? Or herself? What was stopping her from reporting what she knew?

The recitation of the rosary continues, followed by a wave of response. Sally tries to see where Bridget and Margie are but they are nowhere in sight. The smell of incense fills her with its cloying scent. She closes her eyes, listens to the prayers, trying to remember the May altars she made as a girl. Even then Bridget and Margie vied with each other for the biggest bunch of wild flowers they could gather from the fields surrounding the houses.

Sally's mouth tries to form the words that come so easily to the women around her. Perhaps if she had a set of beads through her fingers it might be easier, or the scapulars she'd worn as a child around her neck. She looks at the statue, the once bright colours on the painted face and body peeling back to bare wood. All those years hidden in a tree, minding her own business, then her arm chopped off for her troubles.

The heat and glare from the candles combined with the sickly sweet smell of the incense begin to make her feel nauseous. Sally rises from the seat and stumbles outside in search of clean, May air.

Angels

Sarah watches from the other side of the bed as Gabriel, his hands black as a funeral hat, unscrew the lid from the glass jar. Two long, lean fingers slide around the sides before easing out a dollop of ointment. Its texture brings an image of Sarah's Aunt Rose, who made the best ice-cream in all Galway. Sarah closes her eyes, releasing the breath trapped in her chest and wonders what Rose might think if she were really here today, Sarah herself an old woman now and James, the young man she'd married all those years ago, an invalid.

Gabriel bends low over the bed to finish the task, so tall himself he seems folded in two. He begins lathering ointment as if icing a cake. Sarah, momentarily, is torn between the parsimony that characterised her upbringing and Gabriel's intent determination to keep James comfortable. 'Client', is the word Gabriel uses to describe people like James but Sarah can't help associating it with bankers and solicitors.

'There. All done', Gabriel says, fixing the adhesive clips to the incontinence pad and pulling over James' bare legs and torso a clean pair of nondescript brown flannel pyjamas. Despite coming to Ireland over a decade ago, there's still a trace of the Caribbean in his voice, the contours and shadings of a distant land Sarah can only dream about.

Sarah busies herself placing the soiled pad in one of the fragranced bags that she saw in the baby aisle of the local supermarket. She slips out of the room barely making a sound in her woollen, fur-lined slippers. Her feet get so cold that she has to wear socks as well. As she leaves the room she can hear Gabriel dipping the sponge into the blue basin on the bedside table in order to wash James's face and hands. James will sleep for a while now, soothed by Gabriel's musical voice. She opens the back door, stepping out into a late spring morning. Startled birds, pecking at stale bread thrown on the grass, scatter at the sound Sarah makes lifting the lid from the outside bin. She doesn't mind the small starlings and robins feeding but hates the appearance of magpies, big predators with thick beaks. Whenever magpies swoop into her garden, Sarah bursts out and raises her fist to them, and thinks how wild she must look in her long black skirts and dark cardigans, with her grey hair tumbling around her shoulders. When she goes for a walk or to the shops she sometimes sees dead birds, some of them barely formed, in various stages of decay. Sarah's mother Lily had died in childbirth and the baby, number nine as Rose called the little boy, went with her. There were always so many mouths to feed and so much work to do, washing, baking and mending clothes, they were lucky they had a spinster aunt to come and look after them even though Rose called Sarah's father, 'a cantankerous hoor of a man'. For the sake of the large brood, they soon made their peace and, apart from a few skirmishes, for the most part they were civil to each other.

'I'll put the kettle on', Gabriel says when Sarah returns to the kitchen, locking the door behind her. Gabriel looks relaxed, wearing a smile that strips back his lips, showing two perfect white rows. Big piano keys, Sarah thinks, Aunt Rose again coming to mind. Rose had played the organ in the Church choir and 'Damn good', as she often remarked of herself.

'Thanks, you're an angel', Sarah says, opening the glass doors of the china cabinet and taking out her best cups.

'No need for that, a mug is fine', Gabriel replies.

Sarah ignores the remark as she always does and places a fine bone china cup and saucer on the table. 'I've left some biscuits and you know where the fridge is', Sarah says. 'You know tea isn't tea unless taken from best china'. It's a joke between them now and helped to break the ice the first day Gabriel came to the house to begin his duties.

'Thank you Sarah, you are so kind. Today is indeed chilly but it's lovely and bright. Go for your walk and enjoy it. A cup of tea and a biscuit, that's all I want', Gabriel insists, 'Then I start some washing and ironing'.

'Yes, the amount of washing is fierce', Sarah replies, 'Sometimes there are accidents …'

The word seems to bounce off the faded green of the walls and falls like an unexploded shell between them.

'This place could do with a lick of paint … Not that I'm asking you', Sarah hastily adds. 'You do more than enough already'.

'For which I receive payment from the Irish Government', Gabriel replies, rewarding her with another wide smile.

'They don't pay you half enough. I don't know what I will do without you', Sarah says, looking him full in his eyes which are liquid pools of brown. 'James can't bear anything creased against his skin, the amount of sheets and pyjamas, it's …'

'Neverend … ing', Gabriel finishes for her.

'And yes, a nice coat of Calypso yellow would bring the sun shining in here for sure'. He doesn't commit himself to the actual work however and Sarah does not press the point. Gabriel lifts the net curtain at the kitchen window to peek outside.

'No rain today, I'll soon have those sheets dancing in the wind'.

Sarah admires his broad back. It looks so strong, as if it could bear a lot of burdens. Sarah knows he is a single man, only working as a home help on a temporary basis and that in a few weeks time he'll be taking up a college place, hoping to become a fully trained nurse. She steps into the tiled hallway with its diagonal pattern where she puts on her brown winter coat and ties a scarf under her chin.

'Don't cast a stitch 'till May is out', Rose always said when Sarah and her siblings wanted to strip off their heavy jumpers the minute the summer arrived.

Sarah avoids the mirror hung on heavy silver chains over the hall table. These days she doesn't much like looking at her reflection, opting mostly for the compact sized mirror in her handbag. She can section off her face, compartmentalise her eyes and mouth. Make sure there's no lipstick on her teeth. She wears it because her mouth feels so dry but it's a barely noticeable shade of light pink.

She opens the front door, as always, avoiding the sight of the new apartment blocks completed just a year before. As it is still mid-morning, the usual clatter of children playing in the cul-de-sac is absent. Sarah missed the peace and quiet she was used to before all the building developments changed the face of her small housing estate at the bottom of the Dublin mountains.

A pale sword of sunlight glances off the pyramid shaped roof of the local shopping centre, peeking over the hill at the top of the pathway through the park that leads to its entrance. The Spear of Lugh, Sarah calls it, the image coming from the stories Aunt Rose liked to tell Sarah and her siblings when they were small. Tales of ancient mythology and of times when gods and goddesses roamed the land, not ordinary folk like themselves. Rose especially liked the one about the Spear of Lugh and how, between battles, it had to be immersed in Dagda's Cauldron to contain its powers. There was always a big cauldron on the stove. Thanks to Rose, they never went hungry.

Sarah won't walk too far today. Her bones are beginning to feel the ache of so many cold winters under the mountains in a house that's poorly insulated. And she's been up a few times these last few nights hearing James crying out in his sleep from her room down the hall. She must keep her own health in good order but going for walks just isn't the same without him.

When he first retired they'd go for a long walk together every day and then into the shopping centre for a cup of coffee.

'Imagine Sarah', he'd said to her one day, 'Before this place was built, before we came here even, there was nothing here but a huge field of poppies'.

She sits down on one of the benches near the artificial pond in the park. An empty bottle of vodka is on the ground beside the overflowing bin and nearby, one bright pink shoe. She can almost hear Rose's voice saying, 'Some hussy left her calling card, God knows what she was up to'.

Sarah looks out at the pond, seeing two swans make their way from the reeds. Despite the pond being man-made they seemed happy to settle there. Sarah looks at her watch. Sometimes Gabriel stays a little longer than the two hours he's paid for by The Irish Government but she reckons that's because he knows he's going soon and then there'd be a stream of carers, the good, the bad and the ugly as James himself might say, if his speech wasn't so slurred. She knew that James was slowly shutting down. Sarah honestly wondered how much longer she herself would be able to go through the daily routine of constant wiping and cleaning, the incontinence pads and the worrying if the food was mashed soft enough for James so he wouldn't choke like a baby. She thinks about the sound of James's foot slapping along the concrete when he got the first stroke. How it irritated her until she converted the sound in her mind to the scrape of the plasterer in the new room that was built in the house in Galway, thanks to Aunt Rose's diligence with money and resources. Sarah can still see Rose giving the burly plasterer the eye, shortening her skirts for his benefit and lathering on red lipstick. All to no avail. She would die an old maid she predicted, 'Thanks to these crooked teeth, big as Lugh's Spear'.

When Sarah arrives home with her shopping bag filled with fresh milk and scones, Gabriel practically rushes out the door.

'I got a phone call from the client I visit after your husband James … or I should say, the client's daughter. I'm afraid there's an emergency Sarah; I'll have to leave early'.

'Okay, I'll see you on Monday', Sarah replies, trying not to let the disappointment show on her face. The weekend stretches out ahead. She listens to the news on the radio and makes the soup into which she will mash bread for James. It's a nourishing soup, homemade with lots of chunky vegetables. She makes sure it's very mushy, like the bread and milk with sugar, or 'goody' as Rose called it when she gave it to her as a child to help her sleep, especially on those nights she'd remember her mother and be overcome with tears.

She prepares the tray and leaves it on the table until the bowl of soup cools down. She gathers up the rug for around her knees and picks up the radio from the mahogany sideboard. When James has been fed she'll turn it on, and together they'll listen to the afternoon's programmes. Music is always a favourite with James, soft music that he closes his eyes to listen to while Sarah sits and worries about the future. When she reaches the bedroom door she pushes against it with her elbow. What she sees when it opens reminds her of a snow-dome Rose gave her as a gift one Christmas.

James has systematically torn away at a hole in the duck filled pillow and some of the feathers are scattered all over the eiderdown. Those pillows are as old as their marriage. Rose presented them as a wedding gift, saying,

'No matter what happens during the day, you'll always get a good sleep at night'. James must have found a slight tear and kept pulling at it, eroding the space until the feathers fluttered out like yellowing confetti. Sarah looks down at his mouth twisting into knots at the corners, drool sliding down his chin. She puts down the radio and the rug and takes out her handkerchief from her apron pocket. With one swift movement she wipes his face clean.

Sarah looks down at James and sees the despair in his eyes. Her eyes travel to his toenails. The time is coming when she will have to send for a chiropodist. James's toenails were becoming so thick they reminded her of crocodile feet. He himself was becoming like a crocodile, cold to the touch, his skin scaly, turning shades of mauve if there wasn't a constant temperature maintained in the bedroom. How long more could it go on? For now, it was

Sarah who knelt with the basin and towel, putting each foot into the hot soapy water to try and soften the nails that were hardening like mollusc. When the job's done she gathers the clippings into a tissue and burns them in the Stanley range. They make a sizzling sound, a cremation of cells. In the end that's what it all boiled down to, nail clippings and tufts of hair.

She reaches into the bedside drawer and takes out the nail scissors. With mounting recklessness, she cuts through one of the pillows with the sharpest edge, shaking out the feathers in a flail of cockfight, roosters clawing the ground, Aunt Rose running with her basin full of seed, scattering all before her. Aunt Rose always made everything right and Sarah wished with all her heart she was there in the room now, just one more time so she could hear her voice, nestle into her comforting arms, smell the clean smell of her. Sarah cradles her husband, feathers floating and settling on their bare heads like flurries of snow.

ABOUT THE AUTHOR

Photo © John Minihan

Eileen Casey is a fiction writer, poet and journalist. Originally from the Midlands, she lives in Tallaght, Co Dublin. A Creative Writing Tutor with Kilroy's College, Home Tuitions, she's worked in adult education since the 1980s. Her work is widely published, including *Drinking the Colour Blue* (New Island, 2008) and *From Bone to Blossom* (2011), a collaboration with visual artist Emma Barone, supported by Offaly County Council, South Dublin County Council and AltEnts Publishing (Rua Red, Tallaght). Awards include the Hennessy Literary Award in Emerging Fiction, the South Tipperary Festival Prize, Listowel Writers' Week Short Fiction Award, the Maria Edgeworth Fiction Award, the Cecil Day Lewis Award, the Golden Pen Prize, Arts Council bursaries (2010/2011) and a Katherine Kavanagh Fellowship. She was a visiting writer, supported by Culture Ireland, on the Eastern Kentucky University's Winter Programme in Lexington, Kentucky, 2011. She holds a BA (Hons) in Humanities from Dublin City University and in 2012 graduated with distinction from the M.Phil in Creative Writing at Trinity College Dublin.